Uyghur Folktales

Tales from the Heart of Central Asia

Memet T Zunun

London 2024

Preface:

Dear Reader,

Prepare to embark on a remarkable journey through the pages of "Tales from the Heart of Central Asia: Uyghur Folktales." This collection brings together timeless classics and new tales—many of which will be fresh and unfamiliar to Western readers—that will captivate the hearts of both the young and the young at heart. Beyond their enchanting allure, these stories are essential in preserving and celebrating the vibrant Uyghur culture.

For centuries, the Silk Road has been a crossroads of cultures, where stories from distant lands converged, evolved, and enriched countless generations. In this book, I honour the enduring spirit of storytelling by presenting a blend of beloved Uyghur folktales and exciting, never-before-heard stories. These tales entertain, spark your imagination, and inspire you to dream and create narratives.

As you turn these pages, you'll meet characters who set off on daring adventures, encounter fantastical beings, and learn timeless lessons about kindness, courage, and the beauty of diversity. These stories are more than just tales—they are windows into a world where tradition meets innovation, offering profound insights into the Uyghur culture and the universal human experience.

Whether you are a child discovering these stories for the first time or an adult curious about new worlds, these tales are to be shared, cherished and passed down through generations like precious heirlooms. Join us on this journey through time and culture, where ancient and modern narratives blend to weave a tapestry of wonder that invites everyone to become part of this rich and diverse heritage.

May these "Tales from the Heart of Central Asia" ignite your imagination, kindle a love for storytelling, and build connections that bridge generations and cultures, drawing you into the warmth of a vibrant and diverse community.

Happy reading!

Memet T Zunun

Contents

Preface: 3

Uyghur Literature and Folktales 7

Ketmen 19

Komush 25

Bright Bride 31

Wise Painter 37

Proud Elephant... 41

Koreng and Utrar.. 47

The Weaver's Trick 53

Monkey Princess 63

The Tales of the Fair King 69

    Fair King 69

    First Story... 76

    Second Story 80

    Third Story 82

Oruq and Choruq.. 91

Beat, Hammer 97

The Magic Stone 109

Sinan and Umun..117

The Wise Boy 127

Whispers of Pomegranate 141

Evil Wish 147

King and Shepherds 153

Swallow and Kutluk 165

Man's Due 171

Fish and Fox 177

Brilliant Chimenkhan 181

What is God doing? 187

Treasure Mountain 191

Uyghur Literature and Folktales

Introduction

The Uyghur people, one of the Turkic ethnic groups, primarily reside in a region that has recently attracted significant media attention. This area is known by various names depending on the perspective. To Chinese authorities, it is officially called the Xinjiang Uyghur Autonomous Region, commonly referred to as Xinjiang. Many Uyghur diaspora and activists use names such as Eastern Turkistan, Uyghur Region, or Uyghurstan to reflect their perspective. Researchers and historians may also use older terms like Sinkiang and Chinese Turkistan, especially when discussing historical contexts.

The Uyghur people, with a rich and multifaceted cultural heritage, have a diversity that is both fascinating and worth exploring, a heritage that has thrived for over a millennium. Their history and literature, uniquely influenced by neighbouring civilisations due to their strategic location at the crossroads of ancient trade routes, including the Silk

Road, reflect a blend of influences. This convergence of cultures, a unique blend of Persian, Chinese, and Middle Eastern influences, has left an indelible mark on Uyghur folklore and literary traditions, contributing to a unique and vibrant body of work that includes epics, legends, folk tales, and poetry. The Uyghur people's unique blend of cultural influences is a testament to their cultural diversity. It is sure to intrigue any cultural enthusiast.

Historical Context

The Uyghurs have a long history of interaction with diverse cultures, including Persian, Chinese, and Middle Eastern influences. They established a Khaganate that embraced urbanisation and advanced cultural development in the eighth and ninth centuries. They became the first Turkic tribe to settle and transition from a nomadic lifestyle. Despite the decline of their Khaganate in 840 in the Mongolian Steppe, the Uyghurs displayed remarkable resilience as they subsequently migrated to unite with their fellow Uyghur compatriots in what is now the Xinjiang region. The Uyghurs flourished, particularly in the oasis cities of Turfan, Kucha, and Kashgar, achieving unparalleled prosperity. This historical context, marked by resilience and cultural endurance, is crucial for understanding the evolution of Uyghur literature and folk traditions, and it's a testament to the Uyghur people's strength and adaptability. Understanding this context will significantly enhance your appreciation of Uyghur culture and literature.

Oral Tradition and Folktales

Uyghur folk literature, primarily oral, encompasses a variety of genres such as epics, legends, fables, proverbs, and maqam music. Storytelling has long been a central aspect of Uyghur culture, used to preserve history, impart moral lessons, and entertain audiences. These folk tales, with their unique cultural values and societal norms, often address universal themes like the struggle between good and evil, generosity versus greed, and modesty versus arrogance. This universality of themes in Uyghur culture can help us find common ground and appreciate the distinctiveness of Uyghur culture, fostering a sense of connection and appreciation among readers.

The earliest Uyghur folk tales were transmitted orally, with their narratives deeply embedded in the region's rich cultural landscape. These tales often draw from the dramatic landscapes of the Tarim Basin, the Taklamakan Desert, and the picturesque rivers of the Uyghur region, incorporating local customs, beliefs, and experiences.

Literary Development

Uyghur literature has its roots in ancient Turkic traditions, with significant early examples found in the Orkhon inscriptions, some of the earliest surviving Turkic texts. These inscriptions date back to the late seventh and early eighth centuries and provide valuable insights into early Turkic-speaking peoples' literary and cultural practices.

The transition from Old Turkic/Uyghur to Middle Uyghur marked a period of significant literary development, enriching the cultural and intellectual landscape. One of this era's most notable early works, the Kutadgu Bilig (Qutadğu Bilig), authored by Yūsuf Balasaguni, stands as a cornerstone in Turkic literature. This seminal 11th-century work, composed for the prince of Kashgar, offers a rich tapestry of insights into the beliefs, feelings, and practices of its time, reflecting the cultural and societal norms of the Kara-Khanid Khaganate. Kutadgu Bilig illuminates various aspects of life through its verses, providing a fascinating window into the values and philosophies that shaped this medieval Turkic society. Its significance in the context of the

Old Turkic/Uyghur to Middle Uyghur transition period cannot be overstated, as it encapsulates the wisdom and moral guidance of the era, shaping the literary and cultural landscape of the time.

Another significant work from the Middle Turkic/Uyghur period is Compendium of the Turkic Dialects (Dīwān Lughāt al-Turk), compiled by Mahmud Kashgari (also known as Mahmut from Kashgar) between 1072 and 1074. Beyond cataloguing the vocabulary, this dictionary serves as a comprehensive grammar book that provides deep insights into the phonetic and structural aspects of the Turkic language in the 11th century. Its significance in the context of Uyghur literature lies in its role as a foundational text that shaped the linguistic and cultural landscape of the Turkic world. Moreover, it functions as a comprehensive resource, encompassing many topics, including folklore, literature, the names of people, tribes, and places, Turkic history, mythology, geography, folk literature, and medical knowledge and treatment methods. This comprehensive nature of the dictionary makes it an invaluable linguistic and cultural resource, providing a holistic view of the Turkic world in the 11th century.

During the medieval period, Uyghur literature was significantly influenced by Arabic and Persian languages, reflecting the region's adoption of Islam and the broader literary trends of the time. This cultural and linguistic fusion enriched Uyghur literary traditions, giving rise to a diverse and sophisticated body of work that is still revered today. The enduring impact of Uyghur literature, with its profound cultural significance, continues to be cherished and respected, underscoring its lasting legacy.

By the 16th century, figures like Ali-Shir Navai were crucial in shaping Uyghur literature, including Uyghur literary traditions. Navai's foundational contributions, considered pivotal in Uyghur and broader Turkic literature, continue to inspire and remain influential.

The modern era of Uyghur literature began in the 1950s with the emergence of contemporary prose and poetry and was marked by significant geopolitical constraints. These included political censorship and restrictions on cultural expression, which limited the scope of these works. Despite these challenges, they offer valuable insights into the lives and experiences of the Uyghur people, fostering a sense of empathy and understanding.

Translation and Global Influence

The tradition of translation in Uyghur literature dates to ancient times, with significant figures like Kumarajiva and other scholars translating Buddhist texts into Uyghur. The Old Uyghur materials are often discussed in the context of the religious shift from Manichaeism to Buddhism. This shift, which occurred during the 8th and 9th centuries, profoundly influenced Uyghur literature, leading to the translation of many Buddhist texts into Uyghur. However, most of these materials are characterised as translation literature. Therefore, the significance of Uyghur history and its literary tradition in studying the contact between Manichaeism and Buddhism must be addressed. This tradition continued through various periods, including translating Arabic and Persian works during the Islamic era and translating global literature in the modern period.

Uyghur translations play a vital role in modern literature, providing the Uyghur-speaking community access to a wide range of global literary works. This journey, which began in the early 19th century and gained momentum by the 1980s, is a testament to our unwavering commitment to cultural preservation and education. Numerous world classics have been translated into the Uyghur language, and these translations have not only brought timeless masterpieces to a broader audience but have also undergone revisions and updates, with later editions of some works already in print. This ongoing effort underscores the vibrancy of Uyghur literary culture and its active engagement with the wider scholarly world, giving us all a sense of pride and reassurance about the future of our literary culture.

Despite the rich tradition of Uyghur literature and translation, much of the worldwide scholarly work in this field has been limited, with significant research primarily conducted within China. Nevertheless, translators' and scholars' efforts have introduced Uyghur literature to a global audience, revealing its cultural and literary richness. This international influence of Uyghur literature, which has been introduced to a broader audience through the efforts of translators and scholars, should evoke a sense of pride and recognition in the audience.

Conclusion

Uyghur literature, deeply rooted in a rich oral tradition and influenced by a complex interplay of cultural and historical factors, offers a fascinating glimpse into the Uyghur people's history, values, and experiences. Studying Uyghur folk tales and literary works preserves a crucial aspect of their cultural heritage. It provides valuable insights into the broader narrative of Central Asian and Turkic literary traditions. As global interest in Uyghur culture and literature grows, exploring and appreciating the depth and diversity of Uyghur literary contributions, which have a significant international influence, is not just a scholarly pursuit but a cultural imperative. This emphasis on the importance of studying Uyghur literature should invoke a sense of cultural responsibility and appreciation in the audience.

Uyghur Folktales

Ketmen[1]

Once upon a time, in a peaceful kingdom nestled amidst emerald hills, there lived two princes, Baldur and Keyin, the cherished sons of a wise and noble king. These young princes were the very light of their father's heart, showered with all the riches and comforts the kingdom could offer. Their days were filled with ease, for the king, in his great love, shielded them from the world's woes. However, in the absence of hardship, the princes grew prideful and idle, disdaining the thought of work, believing themselves far above such toils.

However, alas, a shadow fell upon their lives, for one fateful day, a mysterious and grievous illness struck both princes. Despite the tireless efforts of the royal healers, their condition grew dire. Their bodies could bear no sustenance save for simple naan bread and water. The king and queen were stricken with grief as they watched their beloved sons waste away, powerless to ease their suffering.

In time, the princes, stirred by a newfound resolve, realised that their cure lay beyond the palace walls. They courageously approached their father, imploring his blessing

---

[1] Uyghur Hoe

to embark on a quest to find a remedy. Though the king's heart ached at the thought of parting from his ailing sons, his love for them overcame his fear, and he granted them leave to seek their salvation.

"Fear not, dear father," Baldur reassured him with a gentle smile, "for we shall return to you, bearing the cure for our affliction. The journey may not be as difficult as it seems." Full of hope and worry, the king prayed fervently for their safe return.

Thus, the young princes set forth on their quest, their saddlebags filled with water and naan bread, the only sustenance their frail bodies could bear. They travelled far and wide, through forests thick and rivers deep, until they came upon a humble cottage nestled in a quiet valley. There, they encountered a wise and kindly farmer named Tohti, who toiled in his fields with the help of a magical creature, the ketmen, a symbol of hard work and perseverance.

Approaching the farmer, the princes bowed low and spoke of their plight. "Good uncle, we are princes from the distant kingdom of Khotan[2]. I am Baldur, and this is my brother Keyin. We suffer from a strange illness that permits us to eat only bread and water, and we fear it has grown severe.

---

[2] Khotan is a city situated at the edge of the Taklamakan Desert and in the far western reaches of the southern part of the Tarim Basin in the Uyghur Region.

" They explained their illness and then asked. "Have you, in your wisdom, heard of such an ailment?"

Surprised by their tale, Tohti saw a desperate hope in their eyes. Being wise and compassionate, he responded gravely, "My dear children, I am Tohti. Indeed, your illness is grave, but take heart, for I know of its cure."

Overcome with gratitude and hope, the princes thanked Tohti profusely. The old farmer then pointed to a grand mound of earth before them and said, "Behold, brave princes, I must level this mound and many others like it before procuring the medicine you seek. Will you lend me your strength in this task?"

Without hesitation, the princes nodded, igniting a newfound sense of duty within them. "Yes, good Tohti," Keyin replied, "we shall help you flatten these mounds, for nothing is too great a task in our quest for healing."

"Are you certain?" Tohti inquired, seeking their steadfast resolve.

"With all our hearts," they answered in unison.

"Very well," said Tohti. "Work diligently until the task is done, and when you have finished, come to my home in the walled garden yonder, where we shall speak of your cure."

After that, Tohti handed the princes the tools they needed and, with a nod of encouragement, left them to their work.

The princes laboured long and hard beneath the sun's watchful gaze, their hands blistered and their bodies weary. However, they did not falter, for they knew their lives depended on it. As the day turned to dusk, the mounds of earth lay flat, and the princes, exhausted but fulfilled, made their way to Tohti's cottage.

As they entered the warm, cosy home, they were greeted by the comforting aroma of a feast. A table, draped in a fine *dastarkhan*[3], was laden with a sumptuous meal. Tohti's gentle and caring wife served them *polu*[4], a fragrant dish of rice, carrots, and turnips. The brothers, ravenous from their labours, devoured the meal with great delight, each bites a balm to their tired souls.

"Such splendid food!" Baldur exclaimed. "What magic lies within this dish?"

Tohti smiled knowingly. "The magic, dear princes, lies not in the ingredients but in the labour that preceded it. The hunger you feel is the gift of the ketmen, the magic of honest

---

[3] Dastarkhan, a revered tradition among Uyghurs and other Central Asian countries like Uzbekistan and Kazakhstan, is more than just a dining spread. It is a cultural emblem, a symbol of respect and sharing, involving a tablecloth, a mat on the floor, or a table adorned with various dishes. This deeply rooted tradition plays a pivotal role in social gatherings, reflecting and fostering the profound cultural values of the region.

[4] Polu, a mainstay of Uyghur cuisine, is a family and wedding dish traditionally eaten by hand. This Central Asian variant found across Turkic-speaking countries and Tajikistan, is known for its unique blend of carrots, meat, and rice, the main ingredients in each country's recipe.

toil. It is through hard work that you have earned this feast, and through this labour, your bodies shall heal."

The princes, though weary, understood Tohti's wisdom. They rested that night in the old couple's home, and each morning after that, they rose with the dawn to work alongside Tohti in the fields. As the days passed, their strength returned, and with it, a newfound humility and respect for the value of labour.

A week later, the princes, restored to total health and filled with wisdom, bid farewell to Tohti and his wife. They returned to their kingdom, where their family rejoiced at their miraculous recovery. The princes shared the tale of their journey and the ketmen's magic; the king, moved by the story, invited Tohti and his wife to the palace as honoured guests. However, the humble couple, content with their austere life, kindly declined, choosing to return to their beloved cottage instead.

In gratitude, the king bestowed upon Tohti treasures of silver and gold, and the farmer and his wife lived out their days in peace and happiness, ever thankful for the memories of the brave princes who had learned the value of hard work. Thus, the kingdom flourished under the wise rule of the king and the humble hearts of his sons, who had discovered the secret to a life well-lived. Furthermore, they all lived happily ever after.

Komush

Once upon a time, a humble farmer named Tunga and his kind-hearted wife dwelled in a distant and green land. Their most cherished treasure was not gold nor jewels but their daughter, the fair and wise Komush. Her beauty was a sight to behold, yet her love for the delighted world of books truly set her apart. Though proud of his daughter's beauty, Tunga could not help but tremble with worry, for he knew well that such beauty could bring both joy and sorrow.

Word of Komush's extraordinary beauty spread like wildfire, reaching even the grand palace where King Sarsal resided. The tales of her charm and wisdom attracted the king, who summoned Tunga to his majestic court and commanded that Tunga offer his daughter's hand in marriage there. Tunga returned home with a heavy heart, burdened with a decision that weighed upon his soul.

Seeing her father's deep distress, Komush, the beacon of wisdom and light, accepted him with a tenderness only a daughter could possess. She sought to ease his burden, assuring him that she would find a way to free them from the king's demand without ever stepping foot in the palace. With courage and wisdom in her mind, Komush set up a plan that would forever be remembered in their land records.

Tunga, trusting in his daughter's cleverness, surrendered to fate's whims and waited for destiny's hand to unfold their future. On the third day, the king's messengers and ministers arrived at their humble home, seeking an audience with the bright Komush. She welcomed them gracefully, her presence so captivating that even the faithful hearts among them could not help but be moved.

Komush addressed the ministers calmly and elegantly, asking permission to pose a few questions. Her inquiries, as sharp as a falcon's gaze, were directed at the king's age and his many marriages. Despite their loyalty to the king, the ministers found themselves admiring her wit and courage. They replied that their sovereign had reached the honoured age of seventy winters and had been wed numerous times.

Upon hearing their words, Komush smiled a smile that held mysteries and secrets as old as the earth itself. She then proclaimed her bride price, a demand that left the ministers utterly astounded: twenty wolves, thirty leopards, forty lions, sixty aged horses, seventy pounds of the softest cotton, and eighty planks of the cooling board. She declared that she would only consider the king's proposal when these items were gathered.

The ministers returned to the palace; their hearts filled with wonder at Komush's unusual request. Though perplexed, they relayed her demands to the king, captivated by the challenge. He called upon his officials, commanding them to fulfil this extravagant bride price. Farmers were tasked with providing the cotton, a carpenter crafted the cooling boards, hunters captured the wild beasts, and the royal stable was ordered to gather the old horses.

Amidst these preparations, a lowly servant sweeping near the palace porch overheard the commotion. Unable to contain himself, he burst into laughter, a sound so pure and full of understanding that it echoed through the grand halls. Though born of a lowly man, this laughter held within it a wisdom that surpassed the king's understanding. The sound reached the ears of King Sarsal, who, puzzled and angered by the servant's laughter, summoned him at once.

The king, his patience worn thin, demanded the reason for the servant's laughter. Trembling with fear, the servant attempted to conceal the truth, but the king's curiosity was relentless. Threatened with execution, the servant, in desperation, pleaded for mercy and promised to reveal the truth if his life were spared. The king, eager to uncover the mystery, granted him amnesty.

With a voice trembling with hope, the servant explained the thoughtful symbolism behind Komush's demands. Each item in her bride price was not a mere extravagance but a reflection of the king's life journey: the wolves, leopards, and lions represented his youthful vigour; the horses, his mature wisdom; the cotton, the comfort he sought in old age; and the cooling boards, the preparation for the inevitable end that awaited all mortals.

As the servant's words settled upon the king's heart, a great weight of understanding descended upon him. He realised the foolishness of pursuing a union with one so young and bright and the profound wisdom that Komush had shown through her demands. This newfound understanding transformed the king, revealing to him the actual value of wisdom over power or wealth.

Overwhelmed by this revelation, King Sarsal made a decision that would echo through the ages. He declared Komush free to follow her path, unbound by the chains of an unequal union. He released her from the tangles of their destinies, a gesture that spoke to the beauty and power of inner strength. The king wished her happiness and awaited the arrival of her true love, knowing now that wisdom was the greatest treasure of all.

Thus, Komush returned to her village, her heart full of hope and happiness. She lived a life rich in wisdom, cherishing the knowledge she had gained and welcoming the unknown future with open arms. Deep within her heart, she knew that one day, her true love would find her, and together, they would weave a tale of love and destiny.

Thus, the tale of Komush, the wise and beautiful daughter, became a cherished legend in the land. It was told and retold by grandmothers and mothers, by storytellers in market squares, and by the fireside in the dark of night. The story's moral was clear to all who heard it: True wisdom lies not in the pursuit of power or wealth but in understanding the deeper meanings that life presents and in following the path of the heart.

Bright Bride

Once upon a time, in a village nestled amidst lush forests and rolling hills, there lived a skilled hunter named Awut Mergen. Awut was a man of kindness and honour, and in his heart, he harboured a deep desire to see his son wed to a maiden of true worth. Determined to fulfil his fatherly duty, Awut visited an old friend one day, hoping to find a suitable bride for his son.

As he journeyed through the forest, the skies grew dark, and the heavens rumbled with the voice of thunder. Rain fell in torrents, flooding the earth and all who wandered beneath the open sky. Seeking refuge, Awut took shelter beneath a tall, sturdy tree. To his surprise, he saw a young maiden, Sewug, tending to her ducks and cows during the storm. While other girls had hurried back to the village's safety, Sewug remained, diligently caring for her charges.

Curiosity stirred within Awut's heart as he approached the girl, wondering why she alone had stayed behind. With wisdom shining in her eyes, Sewug explained that her friends had lost the grace of attention, leaving their cows unfed and their kindling ruined. The rain's pauses would force them to return repeatedly. Still,

Sewug, mindful of her duties, ensured her animals were well-fed and safe before considering herself.

Awut was captivated by Sewug's wisdom, recognising the qualities of a perfect daughter-in-law. Eager to know more, he asked her what she would offer him if he visited her home as a guest. With a simplicity that belied its depth, Sewug replied, "We will serve you with one if we find one. If we have two, we will serve with none." Her words intrigued Awut, and he accompanied her to her cottage, where her parents awaited.

When they arrived at Sewug's humble home, her father, Kaplan, greeted Awut as though he were an old friend. Awut learned that Kaplan had searched in vain for a ram to slaughter in honour of his guest. Unable to find one, Kaplan's wife had prepared a hearty stew from a leg of mutton they stored.

As they shared the meal, Awut could no longer contain his curiosity. He asked Sewug to explain the meaning of her words beneath the tree. Sewug smiled and said, "If we had found a ram, we would have slaughtered it in your honour. However, without one, we would not kill a pregnant ewe, for that would be like having two rams." Awut's heart swelled with joy, for he knew he had found a wise and thoughtful girl for his son.

In time, Awut introduced his son to Sewug, and the two young hearts found a deep and strong connection with each other. They fell in love and were soon wed, their lives filled with hope and happiness.

Nevertheless, fate had more trials in store for Awut ever the trickster. One day, while hunting deep in the vast forest, Awut crossed paths with the king of the land, who was out with his noble entourage. Unknowingly, Awut shot the very deer the king had been aiming for, igniting the monarch's anger. The king demanded that Awut make him a new boot from a stone as compensation within a week, under threat of severe consequences.

Awut returned home with the deer on his horse and a heavy burden in his heart. He shared the news with his son and his wise daughter-in-law, Sewug. However, Sewug reassured him with the calm confidence that had become her hallmark. "Do not worry," she said. "I will handle this matter myself." Awut continued with his daily life, trusting in her wisdom, leaving the problem in Sewug's capable hands.

A week passed, and word spread through the village that the king was coming to inquire about the boot. The children chattered excitedly, and the villagers whispered, eager to see what would happen. Sewug, undisturbed, tied her hair back, took a wooden bowl, and went outside to the canal, where she began to gather sand.

When the king arrived at Awut's humble dwelling, he found Sewug kneeling by the canal, working the sand into dough. Intrigued, the king asked what she was doing. With grace and calm, Sewug replied, "I am making the shank for the boot."

The king, astonished, questioned how she could make a boot's shank out of mere sand. With a twinkle in her eye, Sewug turned the question back to him, asking, "And how, my lord, could you make a boot out of a stone?"

Realising he had been outwitted, the king burst into laughter, his anger melting away like snow in the spring sun. He acknowledged Sewug's cleverness and returned to his palace, leaving Awut's family in peace. The respect for Sewug's intelligence and resourcefulness was forever etched in his heart.

The village rejoiced, celebrating Sewug's quick thinking and the triumph of wit over adversity. Awut's family lived happily ever after, filled with the warmth and light of Sewug's wisdom. Her intelligence and resourcefulness had not only saved them from danger but also won the respect and admiration of the king.

Thus, in this village nestled among the rolling hills, the tale of Sewug was told and retold, a story of love, wisdom, and the unexpected encounters that shape our lives. The moral of the tale was clear: true wisdom is not merely in the knowledge one possesses but in the ability to apply it when it matters most. As the years passed, the villagers continued to cherish this extraordinary story, passing it down through generations as a testament to the magic and power within each of us.

Wise Painter

Once upon a time, a vast and ancient kingdom ruled by a king who bore the burdens of a physical burden despite his power and wisdom. His eye was unkind, casting a shadow over his gaze, and his foot, slightly shorter than the other, caused him to walk with a subtle limp. However, his mind was sharp and his heart unwavering, and he desired a portrait that would capture his true essence—both the man and the monarch.

In his grand palace, the king summoned the most skilled painters from across the land, offering a challenge none had ever faced. He sought an artist who could portray him honestly, showing his imperfections without shame or deceit. However, the task came with a strict warning: any attempt to disguise or exaggerate his features would be met with imprisonment, while the reward for capturing the truth would be beyond measure.

Among the many, the king chose three painters, each renowned for their talent and precision. With the weight of the king's words heavy, they prepared to undertake this daunting task.

The first painter, known for his unwavering honesty, determinedly approached the canvas. He painted the king precisely as he saw him, with the unkind eye and the shorter foot visible. When the painting was presented, the king's face darkened with displeasure. Though the artist had portrayed him truthfully, the king felt insulted by the stark depiction of his imperfections. His anger flared, and he accused the painter of mocking his regal stature. Without a word of protest, the king's guards seized the painter and cast him into the depths of the palace prison.

The second painter, having witnessed the fate of his predecessor, decided on a different approach. He painted the king as a figure of perfect beauty, with both eyes bright and clear and both feet strong and even. When the painting was unveiled, the king's expression remained stern. He saw the deceit in the painter's work and felt betrayed by the false image. Though it flattered him, the king could not abide dishonesty, and the second painter was also thrown into the cold, dark prison.

The third painter watched these events with concern. He knew that portraying the king precisely as he would lead to the same fate as the first painter while idealising him would only bring about the second painter's doom. However, as he considered his dilemma, a spark of inspiration ignited. He approached the task with wisdom and creativity, crafting a vision honouring the king's true nature without focusing solely on his physical flaws.

The painter began his work by envisioning a majestic scene—a lush valley where the grass was as green as emeralds, and the mountains stood tall and proud under a clear blue sky. A serene river wound through the landscape, reflecting the beauty of the world around it. Amid this tranquil setting, the king stood with his loyal escorts and soldiers, his posture proud and his spirit unbowed. The painter depicted the king with his shorter foot resting naturally on a sturdy stone, his bow drawn, and his eye fixed on a graceful deer in the distance, ready to release his arrow with precision and strength.

When the painting was unveiled, the king's eyes widened in wonder. The artist had not merely painted a portrait but had woven a story—a tale of a king who, despite his imperfections, stood tall and commanded respect. The scene showcased the king's strength, skill, and leadership, subtly integrating his physical limitations into the moment's grandeur.

The king gazed upon the painting, and a smile slowly spread across his face. "This," he proclaimed, "is the portrait I desire!" His voice echoed through the palace halls, filled with satisfaction and approval. The wise painter had captured the essence of the king without diminishing his dignity and, in doing so, had touched the monarch's heart.

In gratitude, the king showered the painter with rewards beyond his wildest dreams—gold, jewels, and a place of honour in the court. The portrait was hung in the palace's grand hall, symbolising the king's reign and the artist's extraordinary talent. People from far and wide came to see the painting, marvelling at how it told the story of a king who, though imperfect in body, was perfect in spirit.

Thus, the tale of the wise painter spread across the kingdom, a reminder that true artistry lies not in mere representation but in capturing the subject's soul. The story's moral was clear: wisdom and creativity can overcome even the most daunting challenges, and truth when tempered with understanding, can shine brighter than the finest gold.

Proud Elephant

Once upon a time, in the heart of a dense and ancient forest, there lived a mighty elephant. This elephant was proud and boastful, for it believed its immense strength and size made it the master of all the woodland creatures. With each heavy step, the elephant trampled the tender grass and felled the towering trees, leaving a trail of destruction wherever it went. The other animals in the forest grew increasingly angry with the elephant's thoughtless rampage. Still, none dared to confront the mighty beast. Thus, the elephant revelled in its dominance, blissfully unaware of the growing resentment it stirred among the forest's creatures.

However, the animals could not endure this hardship forever, and so, in their desperation, they convened in secret. Deep within the woods, they gathered beneath the canopy of ancient trees, whispering of ways to curb the prideful elephant. However, for all their ideas and schemes, no solution seemed possible. Just as despair began to settle upon the group, a tiny mosquito perched on a nearby branch erupted in mischievous laughter, much to the animals' astonishment.

The creatures turned their gaze to the mosquito, their curiosity mingling with frustration. How could such a small and insignificant being find humour in their dire predicament? One of the animals, overcome with annoyance, scolded the mosquito for its thoughtless behaviour, reminding it of the seriousness of their mission. However, the mosquito remained undeterred, claiming that its minuscule size was not a weakness but a source of strength. With great confidence, the mosquito declared it could drink the elephant's blood and proposed a daring plan to bring the mighty beast to its knees.

The other animals, however, dismissed the mosquito's suggestion as folly. Though irritating, they reasoned that the mosquito's bite would only cause the elephant momentarily discomfort. Moreover, they feared the elephant's inevitable scratching and thrashing could endanger the birds nesting in the trees. They implored the mosquito not to toy with their hopes, urging it to reconsider its plan.

But the mosquito was resolute. It insisted that its plan had merit and vowed to bite the elephant's eyes with all its might. The mosquito even enlisted the help of a fly, who would lay eggs near the wounded area, ensuring that the hatching larvae would burrow into the elephant's skin. To the animals' surprise, they began to see a glimmer of hope in the mosquito's audacious plan.

As they contemplated this bold idea, a sorrowful frog emerged from the tall grass. The frog shared its tale of woe with a heavy heart, revealing how the proud elephant had crushed its two beloved children beneath its massive feet. Moved by the mosquito's courage, the frog pledged to take matters into its own hands, though it refused to reveal its plan. Instead, the frog insisted on waiting to see how the mosquito's plan would unfold.

Intrigued and sceptical, the animals decided to exercise patience, allowing the events to play out as they would. Though they wondered what the frog had in store, they kept their suspicions to themselves, unsure of what the future would bring.

True to its word, the mosquito set out on its challenging mission. It flew deep into the jungle, seeking out the proud elephant, who wandered carelessly through the forest. When the mosquito found the beast, it began its relentless assault, repeatedly stinging the elephant's eyes. The elephant, frustrated by the constant itching, rubbed its eyes against the rough bark of a tree. Still, the mosquito was undeterred, biting with ever-increasing ferocity.

In just one day, the elephant's eyes became swollen and bloody, and the scent of blood soon attracted a fly. Seizing the opportunity, the fly laid its eggs near the wounded eyes. Within days, the eggs hatched, and the larvae burrowed deep into the elephant's skin, rendering the once-proud beast blind. Now, the elephant stumbled through the forest, struggling to find food and water, relying only on its ears and nose to guide it.

In desperation, the elephant heard the familiar croak of a frog nearby. Knowing that frogs often lived near water, the elephant eagerly followed the sound, hoping to quench its thirst. But the frog that croaked was none other than the one who had lost its children to the elephant's cruelty. The frog, filled with a desire for justice, led the blind elephant to the edge of a steep cliff. Trusting the frog's call, the elephant took one fateful step too far and tumbled into the abyss below. As it fell, the elephant finally understood the consequences of its pride and cruelty, muttering with its last breath, "All this is the result of my pride!"

The news of the elephant's demise spread quickly through the forest, and the animals rejoiced. They praised the mosquito, the fly, and the frog for their bravery and cunning, realising that even the smallest among them could wield incredible power. Never again would they dismiss the tiny creatures that shared their home, for they had learned a valuable lesson: wisdom and strength do not reside in size alone.

And so, the forest returned to its peaceful state, with every creature, great and small, contributing to the harmony of their world. The tale of the proud elephant's downfall was passed down through generations, a living testament to the ancient wisdom, "Pride brings sorrow." The forest dwellers cherished this timeless adage, knowing that true greatness lies not in power but humility and respect for all. And they lived happily ever after in the balance and harmony of their beloved woodland home.

Koreng and Utrar

Once upon a time, in a charming village nestled between rolling hills, there lived a couple named Koreng and Utar. Koreng was handsome and stylish, always preening and priding himself on his appearance. His heart, however, was filled with arrogance, and he thought of little else but his vanity. Utar, on the other hand, was a wise and hard-working woman known far and wide for her intelligence and strength. She managed their home with care and finances with wisdom and worked tirelessly to improve their humble abode. Yet, despite all her efforts, Koreng belittled her constantly, complaining about her cooking, calling her lazy and useless, and claiming that their improved life was solely due to his luck and good fortune.

One blazing summer day, as the sun blazed high in the sky, Koreng felt hungry and suggested they have lunch in the garden. Dutifully, Utar prepared a simple yet satisfying meal, and they sat together under the shade of a vine to eat. As they enjoyed their food, a flock of geese flew overhead, their wings slicing through the hot air. Feeling particularly pleased with himself, Koreng suddenly demanded his bow and boasted that he would shoot one of the geese down.

Without a word, Utar handed him the bow, and Koreng, full of confidence, aimed at a low-flying goose. With a swift release, the arrow struck true, and the goose tumbled from the sky. Thrilled with his success, Koreng turned to Utar, his chest puffed with pride. "Now, what do you have to say?" he crowed. "You should thank your lucky stars for marrying me. Without me, you would be nothing."

But Utar, ever calm and composed, looked at him and said, "Do not let arrogance cloud your judgment." Her serene strength was a stark contrast to Koreng's raging pride.

These words struck Koreng like a blow. His pride turned to anger, and he shouted at Utar, "How dare you challenge me? Leave my house! I will be better off without you!" Blinded by his arrogance, Koreng believed that Utar was the cause of all their problems and tensions.

Utar picked up her bag and quietly left their home without a tear or a word of protest. She walked through forests and fields for many days until she arrived in a neighbouring village. There, she met an old woodcutter named Arkar, who, sensing her sorrow, offered her help. Utar shared her story with Arkar, recounting her hardships with Koreng.

Arkar, a kind and fatherly figure, comforted Utar and invited her to stay with him and his wife, Sarihan, in their small cottage. Utar, grateful for their kindness, accepted their offer. Though Arkar and Sarihan had little to give, they welcomed Utar with open arms and treated her as one of their own.

In return, Utar cared for Arkar and Sarihan with all her heart. She made the most of their small resources, saving a pinch of flour daily and using the rest to prepare delicious meals. Her resourcefulness and hard work soon began to bear fruit, and their situation gradually improved.

One day, Sarihan, curious about Utar's habit of saving a small amount of flour, asked her why she did so. Utar smiled and replied, "With drops of water, one can create a lake." Her small savings had accumulated significantly, and she advised Arkar to use their earnings to buy a living creature rather than more flour. Following her advice, they bought a chicken, which soon began laying eggs, providing them with nourishment and a source of income.

Under Utar's wise guidance, they established a thriving chicken business, which brought even greater prosperity to their household. Inspired by her wisdom, Arkar decided to shift from woodcutting to farming. They ploughed the land and planted crops, and with each passing year, their harvests grew more bountiful. Utar's determination and wisdom uplifted their lives, bringing joy and abundance to their once humble home.

Meanwhile, back in the village, Koreng had fallen on hard times. Without Utar's careful management, his finances fell, and he soon realised his grave mistake. Overcome with regret, Koreng went on a long, challenging journey to find Utar and beg her forgiveness.

After many trials, Koreng finally found Utar living in peace and prosperity with Arkar and Sarihan. Filled with guilt, he asked her forgiveness, tears in his eyes, and confessed his sorrow for how he had treated her. Utar, whose heart was whole of kindness, forgave him, and Arkar, seeing the sincerity of Koreng's sorrow, welcomed him as a son-in-law.

From that day forward, Koreng and Utar worked side by side, each contributing their best to their family's well-being. They embraced a life of hard work, kindness, and mutual respect, cherishing the love they had found again. Together, they built a life filled with happiness and gratitude, thankful for the second chance they had been given.

Their tale became a cherished folktale in the village, passed down through the generations. It was a guiding light for all who heard it, teaching the power of forgiveness, humility, and the value of genuinely appreciating one another. Thus, Koreng and Utar lived happily ever after, their lives a testament to the enduring power of love and redemption.

The Weaver's Trick

Once upon a time, in a small village nestled amidst rolling hills and lush green meadows, a skilled weaver named Ushtiger[5] lived. He was known far and wide for his ability to transform cotton into exquisite fabrics. With his trusty goat by his side, he led a modest life, making cheese and yoghurt from her milk and finding solace in a warm cup of tea.

However, Ushtiger had a recurring problem - a cunning fox that would sneak into his home and steal his carefully crafted cheese. Determined to put an end to this thievery, Ushtiger devised a plan. One day, his wife approached him and shared their dire situation. They needed more provisions. Ushtiger was required to venture into the forest to gather firewood and sell it in the nearby bazaar.

Taking his yoghurt and cornbread, Ushtiger set off towards the woods, his mind teeming with ideas. As he approached the forest, a bird suddenly flew out from under a tree, startling him. Curiosity piqued, Ushtiger approached the tree, and to his delight, he discovered

---

[5] It means weaver.

several eggs nestled in a cosy nest. Grinning playfully, he took two eggs with him, considering they might be valuable for his journey.

Noontime arrived, and Ushtiger reached the heart of the forest. To keep his yoghurt cool, he ingeniously buried it in the ground and covered it with branches as a marker. He then secured his rope to a sturdy tree, ready to begin his wood-gathering mission. However, his peaceful solitude was soon interrupted by the arrival of a colossal monster, its head reaching the sky and its lower lip brushing against the ground. This hulking creature was so fearsome that its presence brought disgust and unease.

The monster's booming voice demanded to know Ushtiger's purpose in the forest. Remaining calm and relaxed, Ushtiger raised his head to face the towering beast. In a mixture of prose and poetry, he introduced himself as an intelligent and robust weaver, renowned even among monsters. He recited verses proclaiming his talent in hunting monsters and the fear he instilled in their hearts.

In a realm where tales unfold, I stand,
Ushtiger, the weaver, skilled and grand.
Intelligence and strength are my guiding light,

Known to creatures, both day and night.
Monsters dwelling deep within the woods,
Flee for their lives as danger broods.
A seeker of creatures, my purpose keen,
Through forests and mountains, I intervene.

The monster trembled, its eyes wide with fear. It had unwittingly stumbled upon its foe, and regret instantly filled its heart. The beast, trying to conceal its fear, replied that it was the king of all monsters, desperately seeking humans to hunt. It had searched the forest but found none until it met Ushtiger. The monster considered itself fortunate to have found such prey.

Seizing the opportunity, Ushtiger proposed a challenge to determine their strength. If the monster wins, it could feast upon him. Still, if Ushtiger emerges victorious, he will have the right to decide the following action. Intrigued yet sceptical of Ushtiger's courage, the monster accepted the challenge, contemplating how it could defeat a man who appeared as small as an ant compared to its enormous form.

Ushtiger, ever the strategist, quickly realised that a wrestling match was unsuitable due to their vast difference in size. Instead, he suggested a test of their ability to crush the earth and extract oil from a tree. The monster agreed, unaware of Ushtiger's secret plan. They began with the beast attempting to crush the earth by kicking the ground with all its might. However, only a cloud of dust emerged, leaving the monster confused.

Offering the monster one last chance, Ushtiger suggested that it extract oil from a tree to prove its strength. The monster gripped a nearby tree, exerting all its power. But despite its immense strength, it could only peel off the bark, failing to obtain any oil. Ushtiger, observing this spectacle, decided it was time to showcase his strength.

He walked toward the spot where he had buried his yoghurt and delivered a powerful kick to the ground. The yoghurt burst forth, scattering across the land like a creamy fountain. Ushtiger approached the tree the monster had attempted to squeeze and secretly placed the two eggs in his hand. As he exerted pressure, the eggs shattered, their contents slipping through his fingers like flowing oil. The monster, witnessing this, was struck with awe and dread.

Ushtiger's triumphant gaze met the terrified monster's eyes. Assertively, he demanded an answer to his question, "Tell me, monster king, who is truly the strongest among us?" Trembling and defeated, the monster accepted, acknowledging Ushtiger as the victor. It desperately pleaded for their newfound friendship, inviting Ushtiger to be its guest for the day.

Behold, I greet you with a joyful heart,
Pure nourishment is my chosen art.
Not flesh of monsters, nor ghostly delight,
But connections forged an inner light.
Come, let us embark on a wondrous quest,
To find understanding and friendship's crest.
For unity and kinship, we shall strive,
In the bonds we form, we shall revive.
So, welcome, dear friend, to this woven tale,
Of Ushtiger, the weaver, without fail.
Together, we shall explore realms unknown,
With empathy and compassion, we've sown.

Accepting the offer, Ushtiger and the monster made their way to the monster's abode. As they arrived, the beast prepared a rich feast, laying out many dishes for its esteemed guests. Ushtiger, mindful of his surroundings, carefully observed and consumed only a tiny portion of the exquisite food. Evening approached swiftly, finding his way home in the dark proved challenging.

Unbeknownst to the monster, Ushtiger suspected foul play. He realised the monster's true intentions and understood the dangers he faced. Assessing the situation, Ushtiger spotted a large cupboard in the room and strategised how to use it to his advantage.

Ushtiger pretended to retire for the night, making himself comfortable in the designated sleeping area beneath a large window on the rooftop. His mind, however, remained vigilant. As he lay there, pretending to sleep, the monster cautiously climbed onto the roof, preparing to execute its treacherous plan.

Sensing movement, Ushtiger sprang into action, swiftly mounting the cupboard just as the monster began hurling massive stones through the window, aiming for his supposed resting place. The beast continued its assault until descending from the roof, believing Ushtiger to be defeated. Seizing the moment, Ushtiger returned to his bed, maintaining the pretence of sleep until dawn broke.

The monster approached the door in the morning and eavesdropped on Ushtiger's sleeping form inside. To its surprise, it heard loud snores arising from the room. Astonished, the monster realised that it had underestimated Ushtiger's strength and bravery.

With admiration and concern, the monster said, "Hello, friend, it is time to wake up." Ushtiger, pretending sleepiness, complained about a sleepless night, attributing it to a relentless flea infestation that had kept him awake. The monster frightened at Ushtiger's audacity, dared not question the weaver further.

After a hearty breakfast, Ushtiger expressed his desire to bid farewell. The monster, relieved by his departure, prepared to offer a parting gift as a token of their friendship. It filled a chest with gold and silver and presented it to Ushtiger with heartfelt gratitude. Overwhelmed by the weight of the chest, Ushtiger cunningly played his next move.

According to their custom, Ushtiger explained, if someone presents a gift as a sign of friendship, they must carry it to the recipient's home. Ushtiger, pretending to be incapable of moving the chest, challenged the monster to fulfil this custom. The beast, falling into Ushtiger's trap, agreed to carry the heavy burden.

As they embarked on the journey and neared Ushtiger's home, he spotted his wife anxiously awaiting his return. Seizing the opportunity to continue his ruse, Ushtiger approached his wife and instructed her to make a fuss with pots and pans as soon as she saw him and the monster. He further advised her to shout from the kitchen,

"Which monster do you want me to kill to make food for your friend?"

His wife's eyes filled with curiosity, tinged with disbelief. Still, she complied, assuming her husband had a clever plan.

With the monster in tow, Ushtiger arrived at his home. However, the beast could not enter due to its towering stature. Undeterred, Ushtiger managed to arrange a makeshift table outside his house. As they sat down, his wife's voice echoed from inside, shouting the predetermined phrase.

The monster, overcome with terror and paranoia, swiftly rose to its feet and fled. Ushtiger, satisfied with the success of his trickery, shared the details with his wife, and they proceeded to move the acquired gold and silver into their humble abode.

Meanwhile, the fleeing monster encountered a fox along its path. The fox, notorious for stealing cheese from Ushtiger's house, was on its way to steal once again. Sensing the monster's distress, the fox inquired about its plight.

Upon learning of Ushtiger's exploits, the fox mocked the monster for its weakness, mocking its tall stature and lack of intelligence. It offered to help the monster exact revenge and retrieve the stolen treasures.

Cautious yet hopeful, the monster agreed to tie the fox's tail to a rope as insurance against trickery. They proceeded together toward Ushtiger's home.

Inside, Ushtiger had finished moving the treasure and climbed to the rooftop to observe the approaching duo. Spotting the fox and monster, he braced himself, waiting for the opportune moment to strike.

As they drew closer, Ushtiger raised his voice, pretending to scold the fox for not delivering the monsters as promised. He accused the fox of delay and indicated that he intended to punish it for failing. Consumed by fear, the beast interpreted Ushtiger's words, believing the fox had lured it into a trap.

Without hesitation, the monster pulled the rope, pulling the fox toward it. In rage and desperation, the beast smashed the fox against a nearby rock, conquering it from existence.

From that day forward, the monster never approached a human again, haunted by the memory of its encounter with Ushtiger. With the acquired wealth, Ushtiger and his wife lived a life of contentment and prosperity, free from the troubles of the monster and the thieving fox.

Thus, the tale of Ushtiger, the cunning weaver, spread far and wide, becoming a testament to the power of intelligence and wit over sheer strength. It served as a reminder that true bravery lies not in physical prowess alone but in the ability to outsmart one's adversaries, ensuring a happily ever after for those who dare to be clever.

Monkey Princess

Once upon a time, a wealthy man named Turak, who had a beautiful daughter named Aygul, resided in the capital city. In the same town, the king and his three sons also lived. One fateful day, the three princes caught sight of Aygul and instantly fell in love with her. The eldest prince sent a friend to the king to request permission to marry her. The following day, the second prince dispatched his friend with the same intention, and on the third day, the youngest prince, Qarluq, sent his friend to propose to Aygul.

The king faced a dilemma with his sons contesting for Aygul's hand in marriage. To resolve the issue, he developed a unique solution. He gathered his sons and presented them with a bow and arrows, instructing them to shoot at Aygul's house. The prince whose arrow landed closest would win her hand. Curious and somewhat shocked, the people of the city awaited the outcome.

The next day, the three princes stood at the designated spot, armed with their weapons. They aimed and released their arrows towards Aygul's house. The arrow of the eldest prince struck the gate of Aygul's courtyard, while the second prince's arrow hit the entrance to the Chancellor's court. As for Qarluq, his arrow flew far into the desert, leading to an unexpected turn of events.

The eldest prince married Aygul, and the elder prince married the Chancellor's daughter, per the king's decree. However, the youngest prince, Qarluq, faced an unexpected dilemma. Unable to retrieve his arrow, he searched and stumbled upon an old house in a deserted ancient city. He encountered a peculiar sight—a monkey resting on the wall.

Realising this was his destined encounter, Qarluq introduced himself and explained his circumstances to the monkey. To honour his promise, he married the monkey, fearing mockery from his father, brothers, and city people. They settled in the old house, and Qarluq hunted each day while the monkey prepared delicious meals, each one more intriguing than the last. Intrigued by the monkey's culinary skill, Qarluq decided to discover her secret.

One day, he pretended to go hunting but secretly returned to spy on the monkey through the window. To his surprise, he witnessed two stunning women discussing their happiness with their husbands inside the room. They discussed their happiness with their husbands, and the monkey revealed her satisfaction, mentioning Qarluq's cleverness. Overjoyed, Qarluq entered the room, but one woman vanished, and the monkey returned to her original form.

The monkey playfully remarked on Qarluq's failed hunting ruse. Still, he confessed his longing for his family, prompting the monkey to suggest he visit them. Before his departure, she handed him a small bag of bread, advising him to present it as a gift to his parents, as a sign of their marriage.

Qarluq arrived in the capital city, reuniting with his family. He informed them of finding his arrow and his marriage. When his father inquired about his daughter-in-law's absence, Qarluq hesitated. His brothers accused him of lying, doubting the existence of his wife. To prove them wrong, Qarluq presented the tiny bread bag as evidence. The king opened the bag, revealing one of the tiniest naan breads they had ever seen. The taste, however, was extraordinary. Impressed, the king insisted they all try the bread, savouring its deliciousness. Astonishingly, the bread replenished itself in the bag—an enchanting surprise that amazed everyone.

Thanking his daughter-in-law, the king instructed his elder daughters-in-law to learn the art of bread-making from her. When they failed to replicate the bread's quality, the king was disappointed and suggested they learn from her further. Meanwhile, Qarluq's elder brothers grew delighted at the prospect of outshining him in another challenge.

The king then proposed testing their wives' skills by asking them to make shirts for him. The elder brothers saw this as an opportunity to prove their superiority. On the other hand, Qarluq, feeling disheartened, returned to the old house in the desert. The monkey princess sensed his sadness and inquired about the cause.

Qarluq shared his concern, explaining how his father had requested shirts from them. The monkey princess, showing confidence, assured him not to worry and began working on a plan. While Qarluq slept, the other woman—the monkey princess's proper form—appeared and created a thread from Khotan Silk[6]. Together, they crafted a splendid and exquisite suit and shirt, which they placed in a tiny box the size of a matchbox.

Upon waking, Qarluq received the box and embarked on the journey to present it to his father. Arriving at the palace alongside his elder brothers, Qarluq witnessed

---

[6] Khotan Silk, also known as Hotan Silk, is a product of traditional silk weaving from Khotan, a prominent Silk Road city celebrated for its craftsmanship and unique designs.

their failed attempts. The eldest daughter-in-law's shirt was unsightly and missing a sleeve, requiring the Chancellor's daughter to fix it. The second daughter-in-law's shirt was too broad and lacked buttons, leading the shepherd to be bestowed with it.

As the king turned to Qarluq, he noticed his empty hands and questioned his lack of contribution. Qarluq confidently declared that his wife had fulfilled the task and presented the small box to his father. Bewildered by its size, the king opened it, revealing the magnificent suit and shirt. The king immediately wore the ensemble, amazed by its splendour. He commended his daughter-in-law and announced that he would wear the suit himself.

Intrigued by the monkey princess's abilities, the king desired to visit her and witness her cooking skills. Qarluq's elder brothers were pleased by this turn of events, while Qarluq felt downcast and returned to the old house in the desert. Once again, the monkey princess comforted him, inquiring about his troubles.

Qarluq shared his father's request to visit their house and sample their cooking, expressing his sadness at being unable to fulfil this task. However, the monkey princess reassured him and saw an opportunity. She revealed her identity as Princess Aykiz, explaining that she had been cursed by a witch who desired her hand in marriage. She transformed into a monkey until someone truly loved her despite her appearance. Qarluq's love had broken the spell, and now she could return to her human form.

Aykiz and Qarluq revealed their true selves with newfound hope and held an official wedding. They transformed their old house into a magnificent castle, and Aykiz took her rightful place as a princess once more. They invited both kings, Aykiz's parents, and other royal guests to their castle, where they celebrated their love and happiness.

Prince Qarluq and Princess Aykiz ascended the throne the following years after the king's passing. They ruled together, living happily and spreading love and joy throughout their kingdom.

The Tales of the Fair King

Fair King

In a time of great wisdom and fairness, a king of noble character reigned over a prosperous kingdom. His rule was marked by clever governance and just decisions, bringing joy and harmony to his people. Known throughout the land as the 'Fair King,' he took pride in administering justice and ensuring the happiness of his subjects. Yet, a noble quest for fairness stirred within his heart. He pondered, 'Am I truly fair in the eyes of all? Is there anyone who disagrees with my fairness? If so, I must find a way to convince them otherwise.'

Driven by his desire to understand the perception of his fairness, the king disguised himself as an ordinary citizen and ventured into the streets. He strolled through bustling markets, visited teahouses, and attentively listened to the people's conversations. Days passed, and yet, he heard nothing about himself. Determined to explore beyond the city, he ventured into the countryside, eavesdropping on conversations and seeking insights. Still, he found no mention of his fairness.

However, a faint light caught his attention during his journey through a remote village. He approached the window, intrigued by the sorrowful cries of an old lady within. Overwhelmed by despair, she uttered words that pierced the king's heart: "I wish the Night Inspector and the King would die, and the Chancellor's horse would break his feet."

Deeply affected by her words, the king swiftly returned to his palace. The following day, he summoned the old lady to his grand court and inquired about her sentiments. Trembling with fear, the old woman fell to her knees before the king, begging for her life.

The king, deeply moved by her plight, raised her gently, assuring her safety, and implored her to explain the curse she had uttered. Tearfully, she shared her tale. "Your majesty, I am but a widow left without children. I sustain myself by earning wages as a spinner of cotton thread, which I acquire from a wealthy man in our village. Until last Friday, my life was filled with hardships. On that day, a man on a white horse arrived at my humble dwelling, seized all my thread, and swiftly departed. Despite my pleas, he claimed to be the King's Chancellor and acted under the King's orders. Unable to fulfil my obligations to the rich man, he seized my belongings.

Despair filled my heart. Then, this past Friday night, the Night Inspector entered my home and confiscated all my threads. Overwhelmed by grief, I could not bear the weight of my difficulty, leading me to curse them both. I want my thread's return and a chance at a peaceful life."

Curiosity sparked within the king, and he instructed one of his trusted Chancellors to investigate this mysterious rider on the white horse. On the following Friday, the Chancellor embarked on a swift steed, concealing himself near the old lady's dwelling, eagerly awaiting the arrival of the enigmatic rider. As foretold by the old woman, the white horse rider appeared, swiftly snatching her thread and disappearing into the distance. The Chancellor followed him relentlessly, tracking the horse's trail into a dense jungle. Suddenly, splashing water echoed through the air, and the trail vanished.

Without hesitation, the Chancellor arrived at a nearby lake. Driven by determination, he leapt into the water, his loyal horse joining him in this daring attempt. In the blink of an eye, the Chancellor opened his eyes to a breathtaking sight—a magnificent, artfully adorned underwater city of unparalleled beauty. Its streets were teeming with graceful women, while the absence of men added an air of enchantment. Perfect streets lined with blooming flowers, buildings crafted from natural marble gilded with gold, and the delicate sparkle of sunlight all painted a surreal scene.

The Chancellor's arrival did not go unnoticed. The city's inhabitants swiftly apprehended and brought him before their respected Queen. With gracious hospitality, she welcomed him into her realm, entertaining him with delightful music, captivating songs, and delicious feasts. Days turned into weeks as the Chancellor rejoiced in the enchantment of this hidden city.

Eventually, unable to contain his curiosity any longer, the Chancellor revealed the purpose of his presence to the Queen, recounting the tale of the white horse rider. The Queen assured him that he would soon uncover the truth. Days turned into weeks, and as his departure neared, the Chancellor declared his affection for the Queen, proposing marriage.

The Queen, glowing noble beauty, accepted his proposal but presented him with a condition. She explained, "If you choose me to be your wife, I have one condition. If you can fulfil it, I will be your devoted wife forever. However, if you fail, you must return to your home." Overjoyed, the Chancellor readily agreed, pledging to fulfil any condition she set forth.

The Queen revealed her condition. "On our wedding night, I will sleep deeply, and you must awaken me three times." Only those who could rouse her from her slumber three times would be granted the honour of marrying her.

The Chancellor, confident in his ability to fulfil the condition, thought, 'This task is as easy as possible! I could even wake her up more than three times if desired.' With excitement, the wedding ceremony commenced, and the newlyweds retired to their magnificent chamber within the palace. The Chancellor was determined to meet the Queen's condition and prove his love and devotion.

As the Queen's head touched the pillow, she fell into a deep sleep, breathing steadily and serenely. The Chancellor, eager to fulfil the condition, called out her name, shouted with all his might, and even resorted to pinching her delicate skin. However, she remained undisturbed by his efforts. Midnight arrived, and the Chancellor, growing desperate, retrieved a drum and a trumpet. He beat the drum intensely and blew the trumpet with all his might, hoping to rouse the sleeping Queen. However, her sleep remained unbroken.

With the night wearing on and exhaustion taking its turn, the Chancellor finally surrendered to weariness, falling asleep on the ground beside the bed. As the first rays of dawn lit the room, the Chancellor awoke, finding himself back in his own home. Overwhelmed by astonishment, he hastened to the king, sharing every detail of his extraordinary journey. The Chancellor's astonishment was intense as he narrated the night's events.

The king, captivated by the Chancellor's account, grew even more intrigued than the mysterious horse rider. The attraction of the underwater city tugged at his imagination, and he wanted to witness its wonders firsthand. Patiently, he awaited his arrival the following Friday.

On that fateful day, the king rose before the sun, embarking on his journey to the old lady's home. Concealing himself within an old house, he awaited the arrival of the white horse rider. As the rider appeared, the king followed his trail, unwavering in his pursuit. In a moment of courage, he leapt into the lake with his loyal horse, plunging into the watery depths. Furthermore, just like his Chancellor before him, the king found himself in the splendid underwater city, surpassing even the Chancellor's descriptions.

Overwhelmed by the city's beauty, its citizens received the king with great honour and warmth. Days turned into weeks as he revelled in their gracious hospitality, eager to uncover the mystery of the white horse rider. At long last, he shared his quest with the Queen, who assured him that his sought answers would be revealed in time.

Before bidding farewell to the underwater realm, the king confessed his deep affection for the Queen and proposed marriage. Like the Chancellor, he received her acceptance, his heart filled with joy.

As the wedding ceremony unfolded, the bride and groom ascended to their chamber, their souls intertwined in love. True to the Queen's condition, she surrendered to a profound sleep, her breath serene. Remembering the note he had received secretly from the Queen's maiden, the king knew that storytelling was vital in awakening his beloved.

He began to weave tales with great care, painting vivid images with his words, striving to captivate her sleeping mind. At the end of each story, he posed a question to himself, deliberately providing a wrong answer.

First Story

Once upon a time, in a land where adventure awaited at every turn, there lived a carpenter, a tailor, and a pastor. These three companions had embarked on a remarkable journey, going across cities, towns, and villages, their hearts filled with wanderlust. Their desire to explore the world led them to a desert, a vast expanse of golden sand stretching endlessly before them. As they journeyed, the audience was drawn into their world, feeling the thrill of discovery and the uncertainty of the unknown.

The trio sought refuge near an oasis as the sun began to set, casting its warm hues across the desert landscape. They knew the desert held many dangers, so they took turns standing guard throughout the night, ensuring their safety from lurking beasts.

The first to take the watch was the carpenter. He built a fire, its flickering flames illuminating the darkness. However, the journey had taken its toll on his weary body, and despite his efforts, drowsiness overcame him. Determined not to surrender to sleep, the carpenter picked up his tools and a piece of wood nearby, hoping to keep himself awake. As the minutes ticked by, his eyelids grew heavy, and before he knew it, he had drifted off into a deep slumber.

While the carpenter dreamed, the tailor awakened for his turn as the night's guardian. Surprised to find the carpenter asleep, he noticed the piece of wood in his hand. Inspired by the carpenter's ingenuity, the tailor displayed his skills. He began fashioning exquisite garments, crafting a wardrobe fit for a royal. His nimble fingers weaved fabrics and adorned the wooden figure with breathtaking attire. Satisfied with his work, the tailor succumbed to the lure of sleep, his dreams filled with visions of beauty.

The night wore on, and it was the pastor's turn to keep watch. As he approached the fire, he noticed the figure standing by its side. Intrigued, he spoke to her, expecting no reply. But to his astonishment, the figure remained silent and motionless, devoid of life. Filled with compassion, the pastor drew closer and examined the wooden girl. A thought struck him: if the carpenter and tailor could showcase their talents, why couldn't he also offer something?

With profound faith and devotion, the pastor knelt beside the wooden girl and enthusiastically prayed to God, asking Him to grant her life. As his prayers echoed into the night, a divine spark ignited within the wooden figure, and she came alive, a testament to the pastor's unwavering faith.

The carpenter and tailor awoke, their eyes widening in astonishment as they beheld the beauty before them. Each claimed her hand in marriage, convinced their contributions gave her life. However, a heated debate ensued, each one arguing for their right to wed the girl.

The carpenter, full of pride, declared, "She must be mine! If I had not conceived the idea of sculpting a wooden model, none of this would have come to pass."

The tailor, equally determined, countered, "But I adorned her with splendid garments, enhancing her beauty. Surely, she is meant to be mine."

The pastor rose to his feet as the debate grew, quietly observing. His voice resonated with authority as he declared, "A wooden figure, no matter how beautifully clothed, lacks true life. It is through my prayers that she received the gift of life. Therefore, I am the one destined to marry her." His profound insight left the audience pondering about the true essence of life and the power of choice.

Amidst the enthusiasm of their dispute, the king, who had been listening intently, she was stepped forward. The story had enthralled him, and now it was his turn to decide the fate of the wooden girl. With a hint of excitement, he asked himself, "Now, who does the girl marry?" "Probably the carpenter", the king answered his question, and the Queen, who had awoken from her slumber, intervened. Her eyes twinkled with wisdom as she corrected him, "You are wrong. It does not depend on the carpenter, the tailor, or the pastor. It is the choice of the girl herself. Whomever she gives her heart to, that is where her destiny lies." The Queen's words carried a weight of experience. The girl, now fully alive and aware, looked at the three men and made her choice, her destiny firmly in her own hands.

The Queen gently closed her eyes with profound insight, returning to her dreams. The king smiled, grateful for the wisdom bestowed upon him by his beloved. He had successfully awakened her once. Now, filled with anticipation, he began to weave the second story, eager to captivate her slumbering mind again. The story's moral, dear readers, is that destiny is not determined by others but by our choices. The girl's choice determines her fate, not the actions of the carpenter, the tailor, or the pastor.

Second Story

Once upon a time, an unusual partnership existed between a bear, a wolf, a fox, and a rabbit. They had been companions for many years, relying on one another's strengths and sharing life's joys and challenges. However, driven by his predatory nature, the bear harbours a dangerous desire to consume his fellow partners, creating a tense atmosphere.

To test his companions' honesty, the bear approached the wolf and asked a seemingly innocent question, "Tell me, wolf, does my breath smell bad?" The wolf, known for his straightforwardness, responded, "It smells bad." Without hesitation, in a display of cunning, the bear gulped the unsuspecting wolf, eliminating any potential threat to his plan.

Next, the bear turned to the fox, seeking affirmation. "Tell me, fox, does my breath smell bad?" The sly fox, ever the flatterer, responded with false praise, "It smells excellent, my friend." But the bear saw through the fox's attempts at flattery, realising that his meat-eating habits did result in foul breath. The bear consumed the cunning fox without mercy, removing another potential obstacle.

Now, only the rabbit remained, witnessing the end of his close friends. Fear gripped the rabbit's heart, but he knew he had to rely on his wits to survive. As the bear posed the same question to the trembling rabbit, he gathered the courage to give a clever answer, his fear evident.

Instead of offering a definitive response, the rabbit carefully contemplated two answers, stating, "In the name of God! I do not know!" Recognising that the bear might not accept a direct reply and fearing immediate harm, the rabbit opted to gain some respite.

The king paused his narration, eager to know how the rabbit would escape the bear's clutches. Then, "Stick to I do not know", the king answered his question. However, awakening from her sleep, the queen offered her perspective. She explained that the bear would not be convinced by the rabbit's answer alone. He might see it as a feeble attempt to evade the truth and could still choose to eat the rabbit without hesitation. Instead, the queen proposed that the rabbit find a more elaborate excuse to delay his fate. She suggested that the rabbit claimed to be suffering from a cold, rendering him unable to smell anything. This excuse would buy the rabbit some time and potentially spare his life, allowing him to escape the bear's imminent threat.

The queen's insightful suggestion impressed the king, having successfully awakened her twice. Filled with delight, he prepared to share the third story, eager to captivate her attention once again.

Third Story

Once, in a distant kingdom, a wise and just king reigned with two sons who bore a supernatural resemblance to each other. The younger prince possessed an adventurous spirit, full of daring and courage. However, the kingdom lacked a suitable princess to join their family, prompting the brothers to embark on a quest to find one in other realms. The elder brother set off first, but soon, the younger brother caught up to him on the road.

Apologising for his forgetfulness, the elder brother made a proposition. He handed his sheath to his younger sibling, instructing him, "Take my sheath, and I will take yours. If we encounter danger, the sheath will fill with blood, signalling the need for immediate assistance." The younger brother wished his elder sibling good luck, and they resumed their journey together.

Days passed as the younger prince traversed rivers, scaled mountains, and forged ahead tirelessly. Eventually, he noticed smoke originating from within a mountain. Drawn by curiosity, he followed the smoke to a cave and discovered a beautiful girl weeping by the fire. Approaching her with politeness, he asked about the cause of her distress.

Through her tears, the girl revealed her identity as the princess of a kingdom plagued by a dreadful dragon. A young girl had to be sacrificed yearly to appease the dragon and protect their people and land. Now, it was her turn to face this brutal fate. Filled with fear, she confided in the prince, unsure of how to confront her imminent death.

Determined not to abandon her to her terrible fate, the prince reassured the princess, "Fear not, for I shall never leave you alone to face the dragon. I will slay the beast and bring you safely back to your father." Although comforted by his words, the princess hesitated, expressing concern for his safety.

Grateful for her concern but resolute in his decision, the prince requested guidance on recognising the dragon's approach. The princess explained that the dragon's arrival was preceded by distant thunder and rain, followed by a gusty wind. As they awaited the dragon's imminent arrival, the prince requested a brief rest. Aware of his heavy sleep, he asked the princess to awaken him by thrusting a sword into his heel when the time came.

Time passed, and as the thunder rumbled and rain fell, the princess attempted to rouse the slumbering prince through shouts alone. Alas, her efforts proved unsuccessful, and she had no choice but to pierce his heel with the sword. Startled awake, the prince immediately inquired, "Has the dragon arrived?" The princess confirmed the beast's approach, pointing towards the advancing dragon.

Armed with a double-bladed sword, the prince braced himself, waiting for the dragon's assault. As the dragon saw the prepared prince, its fury surged, and it unleashed its suction power, attempting to draw the prince closer. Undeterred, the prince clutched the sword tightly, placing the blade against the dragon's jaws. With a swift movement, he plunged into the dragon's mouth and emerged from its tail, slicing the beast from head to tail, conquering it. Overjoyed with their victory, the prince and the princess ventured back to her kingdom.

Upon their arrival, the king and queen were overjoyed to find their daughter safe and sound, and they expressed their profound gratitude to the prince, embracing him warmly. However, the princess, angry at her parents' lack of immediate affection, questioned their priorities. Puzzled by her reaction, the king explained that the prince's heroic act had saved her life, deserving his embrace before anyone else.

In recognition of the prince's bravery, the king offered his daughter's hand in marriage to the dragon-slaying hero. Festivities were arranged, and the prince was appointed as the king's chancellor. The prince and princess wed, and their weddings became a cause for nationwide celebration.

The prince noticed a portrait on the wall a month after their joyous union. He inquired about the depicted girl's identity and whereabouts. The princess revealed that she was the daughter of a witch with seven heads, residing on the city's outskirts. Legend had it that anyone who defeated the witch in a wrestling match would earn the right to marry her daughter. Failure would result in being transformed into a dog, as numerous valiant suitors had experienced.

Seizing an opportunity, the prince decided to find a bride for his brother. Under the guise of a hunting trip, he journeyed to the witch's dwelling and boldly challenged her. The witch, sensing his audacity, questioned his motives.

"I have come to defeat you and claim your daughter as my brother's bride," the prince proclaimed. The wrestling match ensued, and although it reached a stalemate for some time, the witch set up a trick. She proposed a break, pretending to be thirsty and suggesting they drink water before continuing their contest.

Agreeing to her proposal, they headed to a nearby lake for refreshment. While the prince drank heartily, the witch merely pretended to drink. Unbeknownst to the prince, the excessive water drinking made him heavy, and the battle continued until late afternoon. Ultimately, the witch emerged victorious, turning the prince into a half-human, half-dog creature.

Meanwhile, the younger discovered that his sheath would be stained with blood. Upon witnessing the blood-filled sheath, he knew his brother was in danger and hastened to his aid. After a few days, he arrived at the city where his brother now served as the chancellor. To his surprise, everyone mistook him for his identical twin, treating him as the prince and son-in-law of the king. Even the princess failed to recognise the substitution, conversing with the mistaken brother.

Observing the picture on the wall, the younger brother expressed curiosity, asking the princess about the girl's identity. He found out that his brother had asked the same question before he went hunting. Realising that his brother had embarked on the quest to wrestle the witch, he grew concerned for his safety. Without delay, he journeyed to the witch's abode, discovering his brother's transformed state. Fuelled by anger, he challenged the witch to a wrestling match.

With his unwavering determination, the younger brother emerged victorious, defeating the witch. Pleading for her cooperation, he requested the return of his brother's human form. The witch consented, restoring his brother to his original state. Together, they asked the witch's daughter's hand in marriage. The witched agreed.

"As I am your son-in-law, may I also make a request?" the younger brother asked the witch.

"What is it?" asked the witch.

"Would you please restore them to their original state?" he asked, pointing to the animals in her dwelling.

"Of course. There is no point in keeping them in that state anymore," said the witch, and she broke the spell.

Everybody returned to their original state, thanked the brothers, and left.

They returned to the princess's city.

To their astonishment, the princess could discern the identity of the two brothers.

The king pondered a solution, asking himself, "How can she determine which one is her husband?" "She can ask directly who her husband is," the king answered. At that moment, the queen, silently listening, offered her insight.

"Ladies are often hesitant to ask such direct questions to the brothers," she began. "She should prepare separate beds and quietly retire to her chamber. The one who is her husband will instinctively come to her bed."

Overjoyed by the queen's response, the king declared his desire to marry her, as she had fulfilled his conditions. With happiness, he requested her knowledge about the horse rider.

The queen revealed that she had heard of the king's renowned kindness and fairness, compelling her to seek him out. Aware that the king would investigate the old woman's predicament and learn about the horse rider, she had sent one of her chancellors disguised as a night inspector to his kingdom. The chancellor followed her instructions, confiscating the threads from the old woman to capture the king's attention.

Ultimately, the citizens of the underwater city ascended to the surface world, and the king and queen were wed, enjoying a lifetime of happiness together. From that day forward, no one dared to rob the helpless old woman of her thread, as her story became a cautionary tale for generations to come.

Oruq and Choruq

Once upon a time, a couple named Oruq and Choruq lived in a small village near Khotan. They led a difficult life, with Oruq working as a woodcutter and Choruq earning money by washing and mending clothes, baking bread, and looking after children. Despite their hardships, they saved some money over the years, a testament to their unwavering determination.

One day, Choruq had an idea. She suggested to Oruq that they use their savings to buy a small calf, raise it, and sell it for a good profit. Oruq agreed and went to the village market the next day to purchase a calf. They took care of the calf, which grew into a strong ox. However, feeding the ox became challenging, and Oruq proposed selling it.

When Oruq tried to sell the ox at the market, four potential buyers were interested. They made various demands, saying they would only buy the ox if it had specific attributes. Oruq tried to meet their requests by removing the ox's horn and then another, but the buyers continued to come up with new conditions. Their deceitfulness became apparent when one of the men suggested they would consider buying the ox if it had no tail.

Desperate to sell the ox, Oruq cut off its tail. However, the buyers took the tail and left without purchasing the ox. Left with a dying ox, Oruq felt saddened and abandoned it. He returned home and shared the story with Choruq, who reassured him that they would find another way to improve their lives.

Determined to make a fresh start, Oruq decided to sell their donkey. He asked Choruq to borrow three golden rings from a wealthy man's wife, believing it would help attract buyers. Choruq agreed and obtained the rings.

The next day, Oruq tied the golden ring bag to the donkey's back and headed to the market. When the same four potential buyers inquired about the donkey, Oruq mentioned the bag and claimed it produced gold every Friday. Intrigued, four men surrounded the donkey, and one kicked it, saying that the donkey would defecate gold if kicked.

Ignoring Oruq's warning, they kicked the donkey again, frustrating Oruq. He opened the bag, revealing the three golden rings. Convinced by the display of wealth, the four men paid the desired price. They bought the donkey, believing it possessed magical abilities.

Eager to benefit from the donkey's supposed gold-producing power, the four men constructed a shelter for the donkey, following Oruq's instructions. However, the donkey froze to death during the cold winter, to their dismay. Furious and seeking compensation, they went in search of Oruq.

Anticipating their arrival, Oruq devised a plan to avoid them. He instructed Choruq to tell the men that he had gone hunting and hid in the woods. Oruq entered the woods with his axe, waiting for the right moment.

When the four men found Choruq and inquired about Oruq's whereabouts, she informed them of his hunting expedition. They asked for directions, and Choruq mentioned that Oruq could be on either the river or the mountain. Believing her words, they headed toward the hill.

As they approached the mountain, they spotted Oruq running towards a flock of sheep. Curious, they followed him and witnessed a conversation between Oruq and the shepherd, who mistook them for sheep owners seeking to reclaim stolen sheep. Oruq proposed an exchange of clothes, offering to watch over the flock while the shepherd escaped.

While pretending to herd the sheep, Oruq's nervous appearance gave away his identity, and the four men recognised him. They chased after him on horseback and eventually captured Oruq, tying him up. They brought him and the sheep to the city court, where Oruq's deceit was exposed, leading to his capture and trial.

In the courtroom, Oruq recounted his story of misfortune, and the four men confessed to their deceit. The judge, a symbol of wisdom and fairness, listened attentively and sympathised with Oruq's plight. Recognising the need to address the issue of fraud, the judge emphasised the importance of reporting such incidents rather than seeking revenge, instilling a sense of reassurance in the audience about the justice system.

After a day of deliberation, the judge rendered a fair verdict. The four men were ordered to compensate Oruq for his lost ox, and in return, Oruq would return their golden pieces. The flock of sheep was rightfully returned to its owner, and Oruq was vindicated.

Finally free from trouble, Oruq learned a valuable lesson. From that day forward, he and Choruq lived a peaceful and contented life, with their story fading into obscurity. Their tale is a powerful reminder to report fraud and avoid engaging in disciplinary acts, promoting justice and harmony in society.

Beat, Hammer

Once upon a time, in a humble residence by the river lived an elderly man named Turap and his wife, along with their four precious grandchildren. Their lives were marked by scarcity, as they had only a chicken and an oleaster tree to sustain them. Though they survived mainly on the tree's fruits, the crows often swooped down to feast upon their insufficient meals.

Many a night, Turap and his grandchildren went to bed with empty stomachs as the crows devoured their precious oleasters. Turap tried tirelessly to protect the tree from the clever birds, but his efforts proved useless. Determined to find a solution, he set up a cunning plan. He sacrificed their chicken, smearing its blood upon himself, and laid down beneath the oleaster tree, playing death.

In due time, an old crow arrived, perched upon the branches of the oleaster tree, and sampled its fruits. Spotting the motionless figure below, the crow believed Turap to be lifeless. To ensure his demise, the crow tossed a couple of oleasters at the supposed corpse. Boldly, the crow had stepped upon Turap's mouth, attempting to pluck out his eyes. However, its feet became trapped in the "dead" man's open mouth.

This crafty crow, a saint of wisdom, celebrated the 'dead' man's apparent revival, hoping that Turap would open his mouth.

"Congratulations on your survival, " the crow proclaimed, a testament to its profound understanding of life and death.

Turap, seizing the opportunity, tightened his grip on the crow's feet and retorted,

"Thanks, " said the old man.

"Please let me free," said the old crow.

"Let us not forget that I almost lost my eyes. Why should I set you free?"

Pleading with tears, the crow implored Turap to release it, promising to bestow great fortune upon him.

"I am the oldest of all crows, with over a thousand years of wisdom. As my life nears its end, I wish to fulfil a noble deed for humanity. Trust me, and I shall ensure your prosperity."

Understanding the struggles of old age and always open to learning, Turap allowed himself to listen to the crow's plea. He set the crow free. The crow, grateful for

Turap's mercy, instructed him to follow it into the forest's depths until they reached a majestic ancient poplar tree.

With exhaustion etched upon its worn wings, the crow guided Turap through a small hole at the tree's base. Stunned, Turap wondered how he could fit through such a tiny hole. Sensing his doubt, the wise crow assured him,

"Just try, and you shall discover."

Placing his trust in the crow once more, Turap tentatively stepped forward, and to his amazement, bright lights and melodious tunes enveloped him. A grand door swung open before him, revealing a lavishly designed carpet beckoning him to sit. The crow, unveiling its identity as the prophet of the crows, addressed Turap:

"I have followed the custom of my kind and been caught by you. The Uyghur proverb says, 'If you promise something, keep your word.' Therefore, I present you with a donkey to reward your mercy. When you mount this donkey, you shall find yourself on the path leading back home. Never spend a night elsewhere, for this donkey possesses a remarkable power. Address it, saying, 'Donkey, my sweet donkey, please bring forth abundant wealth.'"

Overjoyed, Turap accepted the gracious gift and embarked on his journey homeward, riding upon the magical donkey. As the sun set, he stopped at a watermill for respite.

"Kind miller, might I find shelter for the night within your humble house?" Turap inquired.

"Come in if you do not mind the mill's dust," the miller replied, extending his hospitality.

Grateful, Turap entrusted his donkey to the care of the miller, requesting him never to utter the words, "Donkey, my sweet donkey, please bring forth abundant wealth," in his absence.

However, the miller's curiosity was too intense to resist. As midnight struck, he could no longer hold back his temptation, and he whispered the forbidden words. To his amazement, the donkey performed a magical trick, droppings turning into glittering gold and sparkling treasures. Overjoyed by his newfound fortune, the miller slyly swapped Turap's donkey with an ordinary one, hoping to fool him. But little did the miller know, his greed would soon be his undoing.

Unbeknownst to the miller, Turap, mounted upon the changed donkey, continued his journey homeward, arriving early the following day. Excitedly, he shared the tale of his magical donkey with his wife, who lived with him in their humble, sparsely furnished hut. Eager to reveal the donkey's magical powers, Turap borrowed a carpet from his neighbour and prepared to display its enchanting abilities before the curious Beg.

The Beg, intrigued by Turap's claims, sent his attendants to investigate the matter. They arrived at Turap's humble home, and with eager anticipation, Turap recited the magic words, expecting the donkey to shower them with wealth. But to his dismay, the donkey stood still, offering no riches. Turap tried again, repeating the words with growing desperation. Still, nothing happened. Bewildered, Turap watched as the donkey produced a large pile of manure instead of treasures, splattering Beg's entourage with filth. The donkey's betrayal was a shocking twist in the tale, leaving everyone stunned and dirty.

As the first light of dawn crept into their home, Turap awoke to the sight of his wife weeping softly. Worried and determined to restore their lost fortune, Turap mounted his faithful donkey and set off on a quest. Guided by the whispers of his heart, he journeyed through winding paths and shadowy woods, seeking the wisdom of the old crow, whose counsel he knew would hold the key to his salvation.

Arriving at the crow's abode, Turap poured out his tale of trouble, recounting the deceptions and misfortunes he had endured. Listening intently, the wise crow hopped gracefully and uttered a magical word, "*Kel*[7]." In an instant, a magnificent *dastarkhan*, laden with delectable delicacies, materialised before their eyes.

With its shiny eyes sparkling, the crow spoke to Turap, "Take this enchanted *dastarkhan*, my dear traveller. Whenever hunger gnaws at your belly, beseech it by saying, 'Open my *dastarkhan*, open my *dastarkhan*,' and it shall bestow upon you a cornucopia of mouthwatering feasts. With this marvellous gift in your possession, worry not about sustenance. But follow my words, dear Turap, do not share the magic spell with another soul, for its magic must remain yours alone."

Grateful for the crow's wisdom and generosity, Turap bid farewell and continued his journey, riding his trusty donkey along the winding road. As he pressed onward, surrounded by nature's embrace, time seemed to stretch endlessly. As dusk settled upon the land, Turap found

---

[7] Appear

himself again at the familiar watermill, its wheel turning gracefully in the fading light.

Recognising Turap's weariness, the miller invited him into his humble abode. The miller welcomed him warmly and offered rest and a place to spend the night. Before retiring for the evening, Turap, cautious and aware of the miller's curiosity, entrusted his *dastarkhan* to his care, sharing a solemn request, "Please, dear miller, guard my *dastarkhan* with utmost care and refrain from uttering the words 'Open my *dastarkhan*, open my *dastarkhan*.'"

However, the miller found himself in a fierce battle with his own desires. Tempted by the allure of untold wealth, he succumbed to his greedy curiosity. Unable to resist the forbidden secret, he whispered the words in the still of the night, causing the *dastarkhan* to unfold into a grand display of delectable dishes he had never tasted. Overwhelmed by joy and seized by greed, the miller deviously exchanged his ordinary *dastarkhan* with Turap's enchanted one, his eyes gleaming with dark intent.

Unbeknownst to the miller, Turap, mounted upon his steadfast donkey, had departed before the break of dawn, his *dastarkhan* safely hidden from curious eyes. Passing the miller without a word, Turap journeyed home, his heart hopeful and determined to rectify his misfortunes.

Arriving at his modest dwelling earlier than expected, Turap considered his next move. Seeking to impress the *Beg*, a local lord, again, he humbly requested a carpet from his neighbour despite the neighbour's reluctance due to their previous encounter. Graciously, the neighbour agreed, unable to deny Turap's persistence and genuine need.

With the borrowed carpet adorning the humble hut, Turap invited the *Beg*, yearning to showcase the cloth that had once bestowed unimaginable wealth. Intrigued yet cautious, the Beg, not wishing to be deceived again, dispatched his loyal escorts to accompany him.

As the *Beg*'s entourage arrived at Turap's dwelling, anticipation filled the air. Turap summoned his resolve and uttered the familiar enchantment, expecting the miraculous display of riches that had once graced his humble abode. But to his dismay, the cloth remained lifeless and unresponsive, refusing to yield even a single droplet of water. Confusion and anger seized the escorts; their rage unleashed upon Turap, who suffered their wrath for what they perceived as a deliberate ruse.

Yet, in the face of adversity, Turap held onto his unwavering belief in the magic that had once blessed his life. Little did he know that his trials and tribulations were indications of a greater destiny awaiting him with open arms in the chapters yet to unfold.

When Turap awoke the next day, he found his wife weeping, devastated by their misfortune. Determined to right the wrongs, Turap mounted his donkey and embarked on another journey to seek the counsel of the wise crow. After recounting the events that unfolded, Turap awaited the crow's guidance.

"*Kel*," the crow spoke, and a bag appeared. The crow then imparted the final magical gift to Turap, presenting him with a bag containing a hammer. It instructed Turap on using the hammer, saying, "Whenever you find yourself in danger, utter the words, 'Beat hammer, beat.' It will bring about a favourable outcome. And when you wish for the hammer to cease its actions, simply command, 'Stop hammer, stop.'"

Thanking the crow, Turap proceeded on his journey, once again halting at the watermill as darkness descended. As before, Turap asked the miller to care for his hammer, instructing him never to say, "Beat hammer, beat."

Yet, fascinated by the promise of further fortune, the miller succumbed to temptation again. In the dead of night, he chanted the forbidden words, setting the hammer in motion. The hammer relentlessly struck the miller, causing him great agony. Awakened by the disturbance, Turap rushed to investigate, witnessing the miller's suffering. In a moment of anger, he commanded the hammer to intensify its blows, compelling the miller to promise the return of the stolen donkey and *dastarkhan*.

Finally satisfied, Turap ordered the hammer to cease its actions, bidding the miller farewell, knowing he possessed a heart consumed by greed. He resumed his journey, accompanied by his donkey and the magical *dastarkhan*, singing a newfound verse along the way:

"When fortune shines upon my fate,
My every wish it shall create.
But those who seek deceit and greed,
My hammer's wrath they shall indeed meet."

Upon his return, Turap devoted much time and effort to persuade his wife to invite the *Beg* again. Despite her reluctance, she eventually agreed. This time, however, the *Beg* sent his assistant and soldiers to ensure the authenticity of the magical items.

Arriving at Turap's abode, they were treated to a grand feast. Following the banquet, Turap showcased the donkey's ability to produce wealth.

Impressed by the abundance of gold and gifts, the *Beg* desired to possess the magical donkey and *dastarkhan*, commanding his troops to seize them. Eavesdropping on the *Beg*'s plan, the *Beg*'s gardener rushed to Turap's side, warning him of the coming danger.

Determined to protect his cherished possessions, Turap stood ready as the troops advanced towards his hut. In desperation, he called upon the hammer's power, uttering the words, "Beat hammer, beat." The hammer sprang into action, striking down the troops and knights, ensuring their defeat.

Recognising the futility of further conflict, the *Beg* and Turap reached an agreement. Turap pledged his support to develop the neighbouring counties, focusing on education and eradicating illiteracy. The *Beg*, now enlightened, acknowledged the value of education and embraced Turap's vision.

With the terms settled, Turap, his wife, and their four grandchildren lived happily ever after, surrounded by prosperity and knowledge. Their tale became a legend, inspiring generations to embrace wisdom and virtue. The story of Turap and his magical gifts was a testament to the power of integrity and the rewards that await those pursuing a noble path.

The Magic Stone

A long time ago, there was a young man named Arslan. Fate had dealt him a cruel hand, for he had lost his beloved mother, and soon after, his father fell gravely ill. As his father's health waned, he summoned Arslan to his side, revealing a secret hidden beneath their humble bed—a mystical stone of great power. With a weak voice, his father shared the enchanting tale behind this precious family treasure.

" As I wandered beside a gentle spring, I came upon a frail fish on the brink of death, struggling in an old, abandoned well. Moved by deep compassion, I gave the little fish a bit of bread and cared for it tenderly until it regained its strength. In gratitude, the fish swam to the bottom of the well and emerged with a shimmering magical stone. It whispered, "For your kindness, I gift you this stone. Made from the essence of seventy-two healing herbs, it can cure any sickness when its water is drunk." Yet, my dear son, I wish not to serve again," his father whispered as he handed the stone to Arslan with his final breath.

Driven by his selfless spirit, Arslan became a skilled healer in the village. He used the magical stone's incredible powers to help the sick, especially the poor and needy. His generous heart and noble actions earned him the deep respect and gratitude of everyone he helped.

But word of the stone's miraculous powers soon reached the ears of a wealthy man consumed by greed. Determined to possess the stone, he sought to claim it at any price. Realizing the danger posed by the rich man's dark intentions, Arslan knew he had no choice but to leave his homeland to protect the precious gift and keep it out of the hands of those who would misuse it.

He embarked on a daring quest, bravely crossing bubbling rivers and climbing rugged mountains. On his journey, he came upon a hurt little mouse, its plight touching his kind heart. Without a moment's pause, Arslan gently sprinkled the mouse with water from the enchanted stone. To his amazement, the mouse revived, its gratitude flowing in a song of poetic thanks:

"*While I searched for sustenance, fate turned sour,*
A cart trampled upon me, threatening my final hour.
You snatched me from the clutches of demise,
Thus, ask of me any boon you prize!"

Arslan answered with equal grace and calm, "No, dear friend, I ask nothing from you. Worry not, for your gratitude is more than enough."

But the humble mouse drew near and spoke once more,

"Though gold and silver I cannot bestow,
As a token of gratitude, my fur I bestow.
When you are in need when all seems grim,
Ignite my hair, and I shall appear, never to dim."

Soon after, Arslan found a wounded serpent lying helplessly on the ground. Driven by his deep desire to help all living beings, he offered the serpent water infused with the magical stone. Miraculously, the serpent sprang on its tail, a testament to the stone's wondrous power. With a graceful twist, it recounted its tale of woe in beautiful, flowing verse:

"A horse's hoof upon me did tread,
To death's door, I was dreadfully led.
Yet, you interceded, saving my weary soul,
So ask, kind soul, and make me whole!"

Arslan replied with equal elegance, "I ask nothing from you, dear one. Worry not, for your gratitude is more than enough."

However, before Arslan could continue his journey, the serpent blocked his path and spoke with unwavering resolve,

"Though no request you have made, noble sir,

I shall grant you a portion of my tongue; I concur.

Whenever you require aid or assistance directly,

Kindle it with fire, and behold my presence inspire."

The serpent then glided away, leaving Arslan to journey the final stretch of his path.

As he travelled, a mysterious voice resonated from deep within the earth. Enchanted, Arslan listened closely but could neither understand the words nor see where the magical sound was coming from. Looking more carefully, he discovered a wingless bee lying pitifully on the ground. Moved by deep compassion, Arslan gently offered the bee water from the enchanted stone. The bee's wings reappeared as if blessed by a touch of magic. It buzzed joyfully above Arslan's head, weaving its sorrowful story into a melody of graceful verse.

"A horseman's whip lashed at my delicate wing,

Grounded and empty, I could not take to the sky and sing.

You mended my ailment, my life restored anew,

So, ask of me, and I shall fulfil it for you!"

Arslan replied gently to the poetic bee, saying, "I ask for no reward from you, dear bee. Worry not; your gratitude alone is a treasure to me."

The bee faithfully followed him and spoke once more,

"Wait but a moment, good human friend,
A portion of my wing, I shall gladly lend.
In times of need, when all hope seems to fly,
Ignite it, and I shall be nigh."

With that, the bee took flight and vanished into the horizon.

Arslan continued his journey, and soon, he came upon a tall young man, his face pale and his spirit weighed down by sorrow. Moved by compassion, Arslan quickly offered the man water from the magical stone. The man's strength was restored, and he joyfully exclaimed, "Oh, noble stranger, you have saved my life! I am forever in your debt and will serve you faithfully for all my days."

"My name is Bulan," the young man continued. "I am an orphan with no family and no purpose. Let us forge a bond of friendship beyond mere servitude," Arslan replied with humility and grace.

Bulan agreed eagerly, and together, they embarked on a wondrous journey. They shared meals, braved hardships, and celebrated victories as they crossed rivers, climbed mountains, ventured through dense jungles, and traversed barren deserts. Their travels eventually brought them to a grand city—the majestic capital of a desert kingdom. Here, a king dwelt, whose heart was heavy with sorrow. His beloved daughter had been ill for fifteen long years, and despite summoning healers from every corner of the realm, none could cure her. The king's love for his daughter was boundless, and he desperately sought a cure.

In a final attempt to save his daughter, the king decreed that whoever could heal her would earn the right to marry her. However, no healer succeeded in relieving her suffering. Soon after, Bulan, eager to seize the opportunity, stealthily steals the magic stone. Armed with this precious stone, he boldly approached the king and declared, "Your Majesty, I shall cure your daughter!"

Filled with hope, the king escorted Bulan to the princess's chamber. With great care, Bulan administered a few drops of the enchanted water to the princess. Miraculously, she was healed, and the king was overjoyed. He ordered grand celebrations to mark his daughter's recovery, and preparations for the wedding began to last forty days and nights.

Arslan was filled with despair as news of the upcoming marriage spread throughout the kingdom. Bulan was about to become the king's son-in-law, and Arslan wondered how he might regain the magic stone. Amidst his worries, he remembered the creatures he had helped and found a glimmer of hope. Arslan decided to seek the assistance of the mouse. Lighting a small flame to signal its arrival, the mouse soon appeared and asked, "What troubles you, dear friend?"

Arslan shared his plight with the mouse, who said, "Do not worry, my friend. Tomorrow morning, the stone will be returned to you."

Arslan's heart found solace in those words, for with the stone reclaimed, he believed he could fashion a destiny worthy of Bulan's deeds. True to the mouse's promise, the following day dawned with a gentle voice summoning Arslan from his sleep. There before him stood the mouse, carrying the stone in its mouth. The mouse relinquished the stone to Arslan, bade him farewell, and vanished into the recesses of the room.

With the stone secure once more, Arslan burnt the snake's tongue. Before long, the snake appeared, its serpentine form poised, and inquired, "How may I be of service to you, sir?"

Arslan explained his predicament, and the snake responded with determination, "I promise you the princess's hand in marriage. But first, I must strike down the traitor, and then I shall bite the princess. Only the water from the stone can save her."

An hour later, shockwaves echoed throughout the city as news spread of the death of the princess's betrothed and the princess's fall back into illness. The king's spokesperson announced that anyone capable of curing the princess would wed her and receive half of the kingdom as their reward.

Arslan presented himself at the palace on the third day, proclaiming that he alone could heal the king's daughter. He was escorted into the princess's chamber, where he bathed her lips with the water in which the stone had been rinsed. With her health no longer ailing, the princess regained her strength, and the king, bound by his word, sanctioned their union. Arslan and the princess wed amidst jubilant celebrations that lasted forty days and nights.

Arslan and the princess ascended the throne with the king's passing, ruling their kingdom with wisdom, fairness, and benevolence. Together, they forged a lasting bond of love, and their days overflowed with joy and contentment.

Sinan and Umun

In a time long past, a young man named Sinan dwelled in the vast expanse of the Tarim Basin[8]. His modest occupation was that of a weaver, working tirelessly daily to earn his modest livelihood. Life gave him little, and he was all too familiar with the pangs of hunger. Every piece of naan bread he got was treasured, a rare comfort in his daily struggle. Loneliness surrounded him, for hunger offers no companionship and acknowledges neither family nor fairness.

Yet, fate had something in store for Sinan. Gradually, his fortunes improved, bringing him a modest income that allowed him to acquire four loaves of nan bread. "It is wiser to possess four loaves," he pondered, "and I shall save one for the days to come. It will serve me well." Consuming three loaves, he set aside the fourth, preserving it for the future.

However, his plans were upset when he discovered all the collected loaves had vanished, except for a small piece of naan bread clinging to the bottom of the box. As he pondered this misfortune, a mischievous mouse

---

[8] Tarim Basin is a large desert basin in the Uygur Autonomous Region. It lies between the Tnegtagh Mountain and the Kunlun Mountains.

scurried by, snatching the last piece of nan bread before disappearing into the shadows. Filled with anger, Sinan hastily hurled his weaving shuttle at the thieving mouse, ending its life instantly.

At that moment, a realisation struck Sinan. "Why should I restrict myself to this corner of the world? I should venture into the wilderness and employ my weaving shuttle to hunt animals!" Motivated by this newfound idea, he gathered his remaining three shuttles and the earnings from his weaving, storing them in his saddle sack. With resolve, he embarked on his hunting expedition, setting forth at the break of dawn. He went across the land, tirelessly searching until dusk fell. Eventually, he spotted a rabbit, and with all his might, he hurled a shuttle towards it. Alas, his aim failed, and the rabbit escaped his grasp, disappearing into the distance. Instead, the shuttle struck a stone, shattering into pieces.

Undeterred by his earlier setbacks, Sinan immediately entered the vast desert, determined to change his fortunes. As he wandered through the scorching sands, his eyes caught sight of a swift hare darting across his path. With a hopeful heart, Sinan quickly flung his second shuttle, aiming to catch the elusive creature. Yet, to his dismay, the shuttle vanished into the deep, unforgiving sands, evading all his attempts to retrieve it.

Weary from his relentless quest, Sinan soon found himself at the edge of a serene lake. A graceful goose glided peacefully upon the still waters, a vision of tranquillity there. Though reluctant to risk his final shuttle, Sinan knew he had little choice. Summoning his courage, he hurled the last shuttle towards the goose, praying for luck. But alas, the goose soared into the sky with a graceful flap of its wings, and Sinan's precious shuttle sank into the lake's murky depths.

Desperate, Sinan plunged into the water, searching tirelessly for the lost shuttle, his hopes fading with each passing moment. But the lake guarded its secrets well, and his efforts were in vain. Sinan sat by the water's edge with no shuttles left and no means to sustain himself, his heart heavy with sorrow as he lamented the loss of his shuttles and the cruel hand fate had dealt him.

Sinan returned to his hometown with no other choice left, his heart heavy with the weight of his misfortunes. As he wandered through the wilderness, fate unveiled a curious sight—a lone donkey's tail lying by the wayside. "Perhaps this odd find will serve a purpose," he mused, tucking it into his saddle sack with a glimmer of hope.

Not long after, his journey led him to an old trumpet half-buried in the sand. Intrigued by its mysterious presence, Sinan added it to his collection of newfound treasures. His wanderings also brought him face-to-face with a tortoise. He picked it up on a whim, carrying it along on his unpredictable adventure. Though hunger gnawed persistently at his belly, Sinan's resolve to press on was unbroken, his mind fixed on reaching home.

As Sinan shuffled forward, a magnificent castle appeared before him, its grand silhouette standing proudly against the sky. Mesmerised, Sinan felt an irresistible pull towards the castle, a sense that secrets were waiting to be discovered within its walls. Approaching the imposing gate, he paused briefly, gathering his courage before giving it a firm knock. To his great surprise, the gate swung open, revealing not an imposing guard but a bright young woman, her smile warm and bright as the sun. Her kind-hearted gaze illuminated Sinan's weary spirit, filling his world with newfound light and wonder.

"Thank the heavens, someone has come!" she exclaimed, admiring Sinan's unexpected arrival. He shared his tale, telling the circumstances that led him to this fascinating place. Her empathy and compassion compelled her to invite him inside the castle, where he could find respite from his journey.

"I was once kidnapped from my father's garden and forced into this wretched place by a monstrous being," the young woman, whose name was Umun, confided in him. "I endured hardships, rising before dawn to fetch water, build fires, cook, and clean as a captive servant. If not for the monster, I would still be with my family, unharmed. I dwell in this castle alone, burdened with prayers for deliverance."

They engaged in heartfelt conversation and shared a meal, replenishing their strength. Rescuing the young woman from the monster's clutches required bravery and resilience, yet Sinan was gripped by fear. Sensing his anxiety, Umun uttered, "Very well, I shall face solitude alone. It is best if you depart swiftly. The monster shall return soon, heralding a fierce storm."

However, as Sinan stepped out of the castle, a gust of wind arose, accompanied by torrential rain. The young lady halted his departure, whispering, "You cannot leave now. Allow me to conceal you in case danger befalls you." She secured the gate, hiding them both from view.

The monster arrived, banging on the gate with great force. The lady refused to open it, standing firm in her resolve. "What is happening within those walls?" shouted the monster in frustration.

"I cannot open the door," the lady quivered. "A human is here, preventing me from granting you access."

"Very well, I shall frighten this intruder," threatened the monster, plucking a hair from its beard and tossing it towards Sinan to instil fear. However, Sinan swiftly produced the donkey's tail from his saddle sack and flung it outward, causing the monster to mistake it for a human beard hair, leaving it stunned.

Unyielding, the monster made another attempt, growling, "Will you open the door or suffer further consequences? I shall send in a louse to torment you!"

"Show me the louse of yours," Sinan responded playfully.

The monster plucked a louse from its back and hurled it into the castle. The louse, large as a walnut, crawled threateningly toward Sinan. Unfazed, he mocked the creature, "Is this your fearsome louse? Do not attempt to frighten me with such a tiny creature, Monster!" In a display of confidence, Sinan produced the tortoise from his saddle sack and presented it as evidence. The monster, perceiving the slow-moving tortoise as a colossal louse, stood frozen in terror.

Nevertheless, the monster, determined not to be outdone, tested its strength again. It unleashed a loud cacophony of roars, each more terrifying than the last, to intimidate Sinan and make him cower in fear. The air trembled with the sound, and the ground shook beneath Sinan's feet as the monster bared its full might, hoping to see him stumble. In response, Sinan seized the ancient trumpet and blew into it with all his strength. The ear-splitting sound disturbed the monster, who feared it would be struck down; it fled in haste, believing it to be the voice of a formidable human.

Sinan and the young lady exited the castle, journeying together toward the kingdom's capital. As they travelled, the young lady revealed her identity—she was Princess Umun, the beloved daughter of King Usun. Her abduction had plunged her father into bottomless sorrow, driving him to the brink of madness in his relentless search for her.

After many travel days, Sinan and Princess Umun finally arrived at the palace. The king, overwhelmed with joy at the sight of his daughter, welcomed them warmly. Upon hearing of Sinan's brave deeds, King Usun bestowed upon him a great fortune, grateful for his heroic actions. Sinan returned to his hometown with a heart full of satisfaction, believing his adventures had ended.

Nevertheless, destiny had more in store for him. One day, a fierce tiger invaded the king's garden, and no one dared confront the fearsome beast. Upon learning of the tiger's presence, King Usun immediately summoned Sinan, entrusting him with the daunting task of removing the creature from the royal grounds. Though wary, Sinan could not refuse the king's request and began to ponder a solution.

After much thought, Sinan devised a clever plan. He wore an oversized fur coat, masking his appearance, and covered his head to disguise himself completely. Armed with his trusty trumpet, he positioned himself beneath a tall tree, playing the part of a pitiful, lonely figure. Before long, the weary tiger approached, seeking refuge and warmth against the fur coat. Sinan seized the opportunity and blew his trumpet with a loud, piercing blast. Startled by the noise, the tiger retreated in fright, accidentally striking its head against the tree and falling unconscious.

Sinan cautiously approached, securing the tiger with sturdy ropes. He invited the king and his subjects to the garden, where they beheld the captured beast and were amazed at Sinan's resourcefulness. Moved by Sinan's wisdom, the king agreed to release the tiger back into the wild, arranging for its safe transport in a strong cage.

Princess Umun watched Sinan's triumph, her heart swelling with admiration. She felt the stirrings of love as she beheld him, standing bravely and confidently in the castle. Yet, she kept her feelings hidden, bound by the conventions of her royal station.

Deeply impressed by Sinan's courage and cleverness, King Usun made a generous offer. He offered his daughter's hand in marriage to Sinan in gratitude and delight. The kingdom erupted in celebration, with wedding festivities lasting forty days and forty nights, each day brimming with more joy than the last.

So, Sinan, the humble weaver who had once known only hardship, married Princess Umun, and together, they lived a life of everlasting happiness and love. Their story became a cherished legend, a tale told across the land, reminding all that extraordinary fortunes await those who dare to seize their destiny. Furthermore, they lived happily ever after, and their love was a beacon of hope and inspiration for future generations.

The Wise Boy

Once long ago, a wise and respected king known as King Kozun reigned. His name echoed through the annals of history, a symbol of power and wisdom.

On a fateful day, an intriguing sight caught his attention as he returned from a long and tiring journey with his trusted chancellors and loyal soldiers. Along the road, a group of boys engaged in a playful enterprise, constructing a marvellous city fashioned from humble mud and grass. Their laughter and companionship filled the air, unaware of the passage of time.

As the king's entourage drew near, most boys hastily stepped aside to make way for the grand parade. However, one courageous lad named Bilig, whose heart knew no fear, refused to cower before the imposing figures. Sensing their intention to flee, Bilig called out to his companions, urging them to stand their ground.

"Dear friends, fear not! I shall personally speak to the king," Bilig declared, his voice unwavering. Bilig asked the soldier to walk around the city. Unaware of Bilig's noble intent, the soldiers warned the boys to disappear, for they had failed to notice the approaching king.

At that crucial moment, King Kozun arrived, intrigued by the disturbance. Eager to understand the matter, he inquired about the situation from his loyal soldier who had witnessed the scene. The soldier recounted the events, emphasising the boy's courage and refusal to back down. Impressed by the young lad's bravery, King Kozun sought to know his name.

"I am Bilig, Your Gracious Majesty, the son of the humble Qutluq farmer," Bilig proclaimed boldly. "I cannot allow you to trample upon our humble city."

The king's face was adorned with a smile of admiration as he acknowledged the wisdom in Bilig's words. Recognising the lad's intelligence, King Kozun praised his courage and intelligence. He commanded his soldiers to walk around the city, honouring the young boy's request.

Months turned into years, and Bilig blossomed into a wise and discerning sixteen-year-old. He embarked on a remarkable endeavour with his trusted companions—a small town nestled in the forgotten corner of the city. Together, they worked tirelessly, shaping the town from mud bricks and various sturdy woods.

"My dear friends," Bilig addressed his devoted companions, "we have achieved our first milestone. It is time to choose a king who shall guide our kingdom with honour and responsibility."

With a collective understanding, the young men elected Bilig as their sovereign ruler. As he ascended the throne, Bilig set forth specific laws and regulations, appointing capable young men as chancellors and soldiers to aid him in his noble task. This act of trust in his leadership made the audience feel secure and supported.

"From this day forward, we shall dedicate ourselves to the service of our people, striving to establish justice," proclaimed King Bilig. "Let our soldiers venture into the city, lending an ear to the suffering and grievances of our people. Should they encounter any problems, let them be brought to my attention."

Thus, the young king's soldiers, known for their unwavering loyalty and dedication, scattered throughout the city, offering comfort and resolution to the people's trials and tribulations.

A peculiar sight caught their attention as they strolled through the bustling streets. Two men, face contorted with anger, were engaged in a heated dispute over a tender calf, each stubbornly claiming, "It belongs to me, not you!"

Curiosity aroused, the young soldiers approached the excited men, their noble hearts yearning to bring peace to the troubled scene. With genuine concern, they inquired about the source of the conflict. One of the men's voices, mixed with frustration, declared, "This calf is mine, but this rascal insists it is his!"

"Nay, that is but a wicked lie!" the other countered, his voice dripping with accusation and the sting of betrayal. "The calf is the offspring of my beloved camel, and this scoundrel seeks to rob me of what is rightfully mine!"

A glimmer of wisdom flickered within the soldiers' eyes. "Hold a moment! Have you sought the guidance of King Kozun's court to resolve this matter?" they suggested.

"We have," one of the men sighed, weariness evident in his voice. "The judge deemed this a slight disturbance and coldly ordered us to slay the calf and divide it between us. Such an outrageous ruling! We were swiftly dismissed from the court, my lord."

A surge of determination grew within the soldiers' hearts. "Fear not, for we shall escort you to the young and wise King Bilig. He shall lend his distinguishing wisdom to resolve this puzzlement."

Guided by the soldiers' confident guidance, the men found themselves standing before the majestic palace of King Bilig. His noble presence shone with grace and wisdom. Surrounded by his esteemed Chancellors, the young king welcomed the upset men.

Once King Bilig learned of the tale surrounding the disputed calf, he pondered deeply, his brow furrowing thoughtfully. His wise question, "Do you have your camels here?" offered a glimmer of hope: "Bring forth your camels, for they will reveal the truth."

Following their king's command, the men brought forth their camels, filling the air with a sense of expectancy. King Bilig emerged from his grand palace, flanked by his loyal Chancellors, and surveyed the scene keenly. The soldiers carefully tied the shivering calf to a tree nearby, where it stood, trembling, as they began to scold it gently, all under the watchful eyes of the camels.

It ensued in an emotional moment. The cries of anguish from one camel pierced the air, its eyes reflecting deep distress at witnessing the calf's suffering. King Bilig, keen and wise, pointed directly at the camel, asking, "Whose camel is this?"

"That would be mine, Your Majesty," spoke up one of the men, his voice filled with respect.

A smile of wisdom and clarity illuminated King Bilig's face. 'By the evidence presented, it is clear that the calf belongs to you,' he proclaimed, resonating with certainty and justice. His fair ruling brought a sense of reassurance to all present, instilling a deep understanding of confidence in his leadership.

Overwhelmed with gratitude, the camel's owner, along with the other men, expressed their satisfaction with the young king's wise decision. His intelligence spread like wildfire, drawing people from every corner of the city to seek his wise counsel and resolution for their difficulties. King Bilig's wisdom not only resolved the dispute but also inspired a new wave of hope and confidence in the hearts of his people, leaving them feeling inspired and hopeful.

One day, the young soldiers found themselves drawn to a man who two boys accompanied. Agony filled the man's voice as he cried, "Oh, God! Oh, God!"

Intrigued by his distress, the soldiers approached with compassion, asking, "Sir, what troubles you so deeply? Pray, share your burdens with us."

The man's eyes filled with sorrow as he revealed his trouble. "I have a son whom I sent to fetch vinegar today. To my dismay, he returned empty-handed, claiming the market had run out. But then, another boy appeared, declaring, 'Father, I have brought you vinegar.' I was caught in a bewildering difficulty, unable to recognise which was indeed my son. Their features were strikingly similar, and both insisted they were mine. It is no easy task to raise a child, let alone two.

Moreover, if their true parents accused me of kidnapping, I shiver to think of the horrible consequences. Stirring the anger of prosecutors and their accusations is ill-advised. Oh, my God! Oh, my good God!"

With concern impressed upon their faces, the young soldiers offered a twinkle of hope. "Have you sought the wisdom of King Kozun's court? Perhaps the judge can offer guidance in this confusing matter."

The man let out a sigh and shared his experience at the court. "I did, but the judge scolded me, calling me a fool. He decreed that having two sons is a blessing and commanded me to accept them as my own. 'It is God's will!' he proclaimed. I was turned away, my pleas falling on deaf ears."

Hope reignited within the man's heart as the soldiers proposed another solution. "Fear not, for our young king, King Bilig, possesses extraordinary wisdom. Let us lead you and the boys to his kind presence, where justice may find its way."

Guided by the soldiers' assurances, the man and the two boys stood before King Bilig's majestic throne. They shared their tale, each word resonating with uncertainty and longing for resolution.

King Bilig, wise beyond his years, gazed upon the trio thoughtfully. "Which of you, dear boys, is truly the son of this distressed man?" he questioned, his voice filled with authority.

"I am!" both boys declared simultaneously, their voices filled with tension. Each showed no regard for the other. They appeared indistinguishable; their resemblance was so mysterious that establishing the true son seemed impossible.

Undeterred by the challenge, King Bilig summoned the wisdom of the elders and his chancellors, seeking their counsel. Nevertheless, even the most seasoned minds could not offer a single clue to untangle the mystery. Then, the young king decided to probe the two boys himself.

"Tell me, where did you purchase the vinegar?" he inquired, his eyes fixed on the young claimants.

One of the boys said, "I bought it from the lady shop owner on the main street."

"And which shop did you visit?" came the king's next question.

"I went to the shop on the main street, Your Highness, but alas, there was no vinegar to be found, so I returned home empty-handed," answered the other.

King Bilig's mind whirled as he pondered the boys' responses. After contemplating, he placed an empty bottle before them, his eyes shining with insight.

"Whoever can enter this bottle," he declared, "shall prove himself to be the true son of this man."

A wondrous transformation occurred as the boys stood on the edge, one filled with worry and the other with eagerness. In the blink of an eye, the second boy transformed into a gentle gust of wind. Playfully, the wind twirled along the neck of the bottle, gracefully spiralling into its depths.

"Seal the bottle!" commanded King Bilig, his voice unwavering. "The boy who bought the vinegar is your true son, while the one captured in the bottle was but a ghostly apparition. Let not the bottle be opened but cast it into the vast sea. May you live happily with your beloved son. The ordeal is now behind you."

A chorus of astonishment filled the air as everyone present marvelled at King Bilig's wisdom. His wisdom had illuminated the path, bringing clarity to the complex case. Hearts overflowed with admiration for the young king; his name would forever be synonymous with wisdom and discernment. Thus, the tale spread far and wide, inspiring generations with the timeless power of sharp judgment and the triumph of justice.

Across the realm, word of King Bilig's wisdom and benevolence reached the ears of King Kozun, who sought to test the young "king's" determination. Enraged by the notion that King Bilig had established his laws, recruited soldiers, and even set up a court to dispense justice, King Kozun resolved to confront him. "Bring Bilig to my palace," he orders. "I shall punish him; whether he enters my palace or not, he approaches me with his face turned forward or backward. Furthermore, I shall punish him if he dares to utter more than one word in response to my questions." The order was swiftly delivered to King Bilig, and the young king had no choice but to follow King Kozun's summons.

King Bilig, accompanied by a loyal friend, arrived at the palace the following day. Standing at the threshold, he placed one foot inside the palace while keeping the other outside.

"Why don't you enter? " King asked.

"Order," Bilig promptly responded.

"You may enter now," King allowed him to enter.

As he entered, he moved sideways, with one shoulder leading the way. King Bilig's demeanour, though seemingly impolite toward King Kozun, was a testament to his unwavering obedience. Despite it all, he greeted the reigning king with the utmost respect.

Angry with King Bilig's unconventional entry, King Kozun thundered, "Who taught you to enter the palace in such a manner?"

With unyielding bravery, Bilig replied, "Order."

The king realised his folly and sought to test the young king's wisdom again. "By what means do kingdoms flourish and thrive?" he inquired.

"Justice," Bilig promptly responded.

"And by what means are kingdoms brought to ruin?"

"Oppression," Bilig declared without hesitation.

Puzzled, King Kozun demanded an explanation.

With courage in his voice, Bilig replied, "Order."

The young king's shrewdness struck him, and he remembered his decree: "*I shall punish him if he dares to utter more than two sentences in response to my questions."* Left with no choice but to dismiss his charge, King Kozun came to a profound realisation.

"The prosperity and growth of a kingdom rest upon the just treatment of its people," Bilig began to explain, his words flowing with clarity. "If a king governs with justice, the kingdom shall flourish and thrive. However, should the king choose the path of tyranny, inflicting violence and causing misery, the kingdom will inevitably crumble, destined for a swift demise."

As Bilig's wisdom unfolded, King Kozun rose from his seat and descended to meet him. He kissed Bilig's forehead tenderly and spoke with heartfelt admiration, "Bravo, young man! Your wisdom shines brightly, and I glimpse a future filled with promise. You will receive the finest education and guidance, for you possess the potential to shape a brilliant destiny. I pledge my unwavering support to you." The blessings of King Kozun, a blessing bestowed by fate, showered Bilig, and the people rejoiced, celebrating the young king's destined role in the kingdom.

With great benevolence, King Kozun, heeding the call of destiny, entrusted Bilig to a prestigious government-funded school, ensuring that he received a comprehensive education befitting his remarkable potential.

Whispers of Pomegranate

Once upon a time, in a distant kingdom nestled amidst the expansive desert, there reigned a wise and renowned king named Beglen. His subjects esteemed him as a just ruler, blessed with strength, bravery, and wisdom. King Beglen, accompanied by a select group of court officers, often embarked on a summer retreat from his capital city of Kashgar [9] to a serene place near the magnificent Karakorum [10]. With a deep fondness for hunting and archery, he revelled in the great outdoors.

A sunny summer afternoon unfolded under the scorching sun of Taklamakan, its golden rays painting the land with warmth. The king and his companions embarked on their journey to the summer retreat on this day. As the weary travellers took to rest the following day, the king, driven by his adventurous spirit, ventured out alone into the wilderness, abandoning even the presence of a servant. Engaged in pursuing a hare, he found himself wandering through the vast desert, overcome by an unquenchable thirst.

---

[9] Kashgar is located at the Taklamakan Desert's edge and in the Tarim Basin's far western reaches. It

[10] A mountain range in Central Asia, extending across northern Pakistan, southern Uyghur Region China, and eastern Afghanistan, known for its rugged terrain and high peaks, including K2.

After an eternity, the king stumbled upon an orchard amidst the desert's arid expanse. However, its once grand walls now lay in ruins, bearing the weight of time's passage. King Beglen's heart was filled with joy at the sight despite the orchard's ruined state. Dismounting his horse, he grasped the reins with one hand and followed a tattered rope that led him to what appeared to be an old wooden gate. Ignoring the orchard's condition, his thirst drove him to shout at the entrance.

"Is anyone there?"

Suddenly, an old man named Soghun emerged from a hidden corner. His surprise was evident as he beheld the noble figure astride a horse.

"Who goes there?" called out Soghun from within the orchard.

King Beglen greeted the old man politely, who approached him with equal respect. With great humility, the king implored, "Please, extend to me your kind service and provide me with something to quench my thirst."

"Certainly, sir," replied Soghun without hesitation.

The old man plucked two ripe pomegranates from the orchard and presented them to the king. King Beglen eagerly ate the juicy fruits and pondered, "As the ruler of this land, why do I not possess such sweet pomegranates in my orchard? Instead, it is this humble old man who cultivates them. This is an injustice. Let me see what this old man can do if I move his pomegranate tree to my orchard." The king's thirst remained unquenched despite two pomegranates prompting him to request more from Soghun. The old man once again plucked two pomegranates and offered them to the king. However, the pomegranates were bitter and sour, to the king's dismay. Filled with outrage, he criticised the old man, his voice resonating with arrogance and entitlement.

"Why did you not bring me the same pomegranates as before?" he exclaimed.

"I apologise, sir, but they are indeed the same as before," replied Soghun earnestly.

"If they are the same, why do they taste different? The first ones were sweet, but these are sour and bitter!" the king demanded, his voice resonating with frustration.

"Sir, I possess only one pomegranate tree, and I picked all of them from that tree," explained Soghun with utmost sincerity.

"You dare call me a liar!" the king thundered at Soghun.

"If I have spoken falsely, sir, it is not due to any deceit on my part. Rather, your desires have transformed the sweet into sour and bitter," responded Soghun politely.

Startled by the old man's wisdom, the king was compelled to reconsider his judgment regarding the pomegranates. Rising from his seat, he thanked Soghun for the pomegranates bestowed upon him from the heavenly orchard. In turn, the old man extended an invitation to the king, urging him to explore the beauty of his orchard. Curiosity piqued, King Beglen ventured deeper into the orchard, marvelling at the abundance of delicious fruits and the enchanting aroma of peaches and grapes floating through the air. Despite the surrounding desert, the orchard thrived with various fruits and even harboured many bird species. The king's heart was filled with a newfound respect for the old man and his wisdom.

As King Beglen and Soghun strolled through the orchard, engaged in pleasant conversation about the marvels that surrounded them, the king, overwhelmed by admiration for the orchard's splendour, extended an offer to Soghun, suggesting he become the royal gardener in his orchard. However, Soghun, with the utmost politeness, declined the king's proposition. The visit ended, and as King Beglen reflected on the knowledge gained from Soghun and the sheer beauty of the orchard, he realised the importance of his royal gardener learning from the old man's expertise. The fruits, trees, and flowers in Soghun's orchard far surpassed those within his domain.

Promising to send his gardener to learn the art of gardening from the wise old man upon his return, King Beglen expressed profound gratitude to Soghun, bid him farewell, and continued his journey back to his camp. He was forever changed by the encounter with the humble orchard and its wisdom. His heart was filled with humility and respect for the old man.

The sun dipped low as the king rode away, casting a golden glow over the orchard to bless the lessons learned that day. From that moment on, King Beglen ruled his kingdom with a gentler hand, always remembering the quiet strength of the old gardener who tended not just to trees but to the land's soul. And it is said that under his reign, the orchards grew lush and bountiful. The kingdom flourished, for the king had learned that true wisdom often blooms in the most unassuming places, tended by those who work with love and patience. And so, the tale of King Beglen and the humble orchard was told for generations, reminding all who heard it that greatness lies not in grand palaces but in the simple and honest labour of the heart.

Evil Wish

Once upon a time, in a land veiled by the mists of time, there dwelled an elderly couple. Throughout their youthful days, they laboured under the service of a wealthy landlord. They earned a living out of a meagre existence. However, as the weight of age pressed upon their weary frames, they could no longer bear the burdens placed upon them. The cruel landlord, lacking compassion, cast them out from the humble hut they once called home. With no family to look after them and no place to call home, the poor old man and woman, despite their troubles, gathered their courage and made a choice that would shape their destiny.

With hearts weighed down and hope flickering like a faraway candle, they turned away from the bustling city and set sights on the distant mountains. There, a lonely cave became their shelter, where they survived on rainwater and the meagre roots of wild plants. Days turned into months, and their frail bodies grew weaker with each passing day. The old woman soon fell ill, her strength fading. In their darkest moments, they raised tearful eyes to the heavens, praying desperately for mercy and a glimmer of relief from their suffering.

"Oh, divine Creator, have you turned a blind eye to our suffering?" they cried out, voices trembling with sorrow. "Why have you left us adrift in this sea of loneliness? What wrongs have we done to deserve such a fate? Please, show us a glimmer of mercy," they implored, their words carried by the wind into the silent sky.

Their heartfelt cries echoed through the mountains and stirred the trees' souls. Hearing their plea, the benevolent God decided to offer them respite.

"Very well," spoke the compassionate voice of God, "I shall grant you three wishes. One shall be granted to the woman and two to the old man. However, you must discuss and reach a united decision before I fulfil your desires."

Deep in thought, the old man and woman began their deliberations, united in their plight.

"Let us wish for the mountains to turn into gold," proposed the old woman, her eyes gleaming with dreams of boundless riches.

"Nay, dear wife, that is a pursuit beyond our humble means," reasoned the old man. "Let my wish be for a piece of fertile land where we may till the soil and quench our thirst with its bountiful waters. Moreover, for you, my love, let your wish be for a gentle cow whose milk shall nourish us. We shall find sustenance and contentment in toiling upon our land."

"But work, dear husband? Nay, I have suffered enough," countered the old woman with a flicker of cheekiness. "I seek not to labour but to enjoy the comforts of royalty. Let my wish be to become a beautiful girl, adored by the prince, who will whisk me away to his palace, where I shall enjoy fortune and luxury."

The wise and aware of their trials and lessons learned, the old man attempted to persuade his wife. Yet, her desires remained unyielding, and in her stubbornness, she stormed out of the cave and ventured forth alone.

Left alone with a heart heavy with disappointment and anger, the old man pondered his options. Frustration enveloped him, and he uttered his first wish with a bitter edge.

"O divine One, let my woman revert to her former state, an old woman once more!"

At that moment, the most beautiful girl in the world transformed into an old woman, losing the prince's affection. The prince, bewildered and dismayed, commanded her to depart from his presence, his voice dripping with disdain. Castaway, the old woman roamed until she returned before the old man. Tears streamed down her weathered cheeks, but his fury remained unyielding.

"No more mercy shall be bestowed upon you! We are but pawns in the hands of fate, and your pride and greed have brought this upon us," declared the old man sternly. With determination etched upon his face, he retreated to the sanctuary of their cave on the hill. Overwhelmed by regret, the old woman followed her husband, seeking solace within their humble abode.

In a twist of fate, their final wish rang forth.

"O merciful Creator, grant us a life of abundance and ease, where our needs are met," entreated the old man.

Furthermore, behold, a wondrous sight unfolded before their eyes. A charming cottage materialised, nestled amidst the beauty of nature. A lush garden, teeming with a bounty of fruits, flourished behind the house while a cow, its calf, and a handful of chickens graced the front yard. Adjacent to the garden lay a fertile plot of land, ready to receive the old man's tender care. The cottage rested serenely beside a murmuring stream, drawing its life force from the nearby mountains.

From that moment forth, the old man and his wife found solace and happiness within the walls of their humble cottage. The old woman tended to the cows and chickens, finding fulfilment in her newfound role, while the old man nurtured the land, sowing the seeds of sustenance. Together, they traversed the remaining chapters of their lives, wrapped in harmony and happiness. Thus, their tale is a testament to the power of humility, the consequences of unchecked desires, and the boundless mercy of fate.

King and Shepherds

Once upon a time, in a distant land, there dwelled an elderly man named Aman, blessed with three sons: Badur, Esen, and Ayuk. As age weighed heavily upon him, the old man fell gravely ill, sensing that his days were ending. Gathering his sons around him, he spoke with a weak but determined voice:

"Beloved sons, my health declines with each passing moment, and I fear my end is near. It would bring me great peace if you could settle the matter of my possessions before I depart this world. Tell me, which among you seeks my blessings and which covets my earthly treasures?"

Silence enveloped the room momentarily as the sons pondered their father's words. Eventually, Ayuk, the youngest of the three, stood up with a humble heart.

"Dear father," he said softly, "your good wishes are all I desire. Material possessions are less valuable than the love and kindness you have bestowed upon us."

In contrast, the other two brothers expressed their desire for an inheritance, driven by their thirst for wealth and prosperity. Aware of their intentions, Aman divided his possessions into two equal portions, granting them to his elder sons. Turning to Ayuk, he spoke tenderly:

"Oh, my dear son, I have no material wealth to offer you. However, let it be known that our family holds a saying close to our hearts: 'Best wishes bring you happiness.' I fervently wish you happiness and abundant blessings throughout your life."

With heavy hearts, the family bid farewell to their ailing father, who soon passed away, leaving behind a world of wealth for Badur and Esen.

Consumed by their newfound riches, the two elder brothers indulged in reckless spending, wasting their fortunes without care. Meanwhile, Ayuk sought employment in the household of a wealthy man, earning his livelihood through honest work.

One day, longing for his brothers' companionship, Ayuk visited their abundant abode. He was greeted as a stranger, to his dismay, and his brothers showed no recognition or kinship. Deeply saddened but harbouring no ill will, Ayuk kept his silence. Time passed, and Ayuk made another attempt to connect with his brothers, only to discover that their lives had crumbled into misery. Esen had become homeless, while Badur resorted to begging on the streets.

Moved by their difficulty, Ayuk approached his brothers with a proposal born from his compassionate heart.

"Brothers, seeing you in such dreadful circumstances pains me deeply. Let us not subject ourselves to the pitying gazes of others. Our family name was highly regarded in Kashgar, where our father's wisdom and guidance were cherished. If you agree, let us leave this place behind and seek a fresh start elsewhere."

His words resonated with truth, and Ayuk's brothers accepted. Together, they got on a journey, leaving their hometown behind. Weeks became a weary pilgrimage until they finally arrived at the outskirts of a kingdom known as Khotan.

As twilight cast its gentle embrace, the three brothers arrived at a humble village named Arish, nestled beneath a canopy of trees. Weary and searching for respite, they stumbled upon a grand house surrounded by verdant beauty. With hope in their hearts, they knocked on the door, their voices filled with humility.

"We are three brothers from Kashgar, orphaned by the loss of our beloved parents. We set forth to seek suitable employment and have travelled far. I am called Esen, and these are my brothers, Badur and Ayuk. We pray you, kind sir, for shelter this night, and it would bring us immeasurable joy if you could grant us such kindness."

The house owner, a man named Ewlik, welcomed them warmly and inquired about their origins and family. He then shared his story, revealing himself as the owner of a thriving flock of three hundred sheep and goats.

"Would you not consider staying here and becoming shepherds under my employ? I assure you, the work will satisfy you," Ewlik proposed, extending an opportunity for a fresh start.

Grateful for his generosity, the three brothers accepted his offer and began their days as shepherds under Ewlik's guidance. In this new chapter of their lives, they would tend to the flock alongside the villagers, finding solace in Ewlik's tales of a fabled princess named Alma.

Princess Alma radiated beauty within the kingdom's walls, reaching the world's farthest corners. Many princes sought her hand in marriage, and the king, in his discernment, devised a test. A staircase with eighty steps was constructed, and the king proclaimed that only the one who could ride their horse to the top and retrieve the ring from the princess's hand would earn the right to marry her.

News of this grand challenge spread far and wide, captivating the attention of countless suitors. Ewlik, known for his captivating storytelling, shared these tales with the brothers during their evenings together. One day, his voice tinged with sadness, Ewlik spoke of a valiant knight on a silver horse who had ascended to the sixteenth step but had yet to win the princess's favour.

Upon hearing this, curiosity awakened within Esen and Badur, compelling them to venture into the city to witness the spectacle. They entrusted Ayuk with the care of the flock and departed, returning late that evening to share the day's events. The cycle repeated, their eagerness driving them back to the city, each time bringing news of princes advancing further up the staircase.

With each passing day, the brothers grew unhappy, fearing the princess would be lost forever. Meanwhile, Ayuk, ever the observer, listened silently to their mourning. Little did they know that fate had a different plan for him.

"Today, a prince reached the twenties step," they lamented. "Tomorrow, another will ascend to the fortieth and soon the sixtieth. The princess will be taken from our sight forever."

Undeterred, the brothers set forth again the following day, leaving Ayuk to tend to the flock. As the noonday sun warmed his weary bones, Ayuk felt a sudden weariness overtake him, lulling him into a deep sleep. In the realm of dreams, his father materialised once more, this time bestowing him the gift of a white stallion. Ayuk awoke to find the old man with the snowy beard standing before him.

"Where have your brothers gone?" the old man inquired.

"They have departed to the city," Ayuk replied.

"And you, my dear son, will you not follow in their footsteps?" asked the old man, his voice gentle and kind.

With steadfast determination, Ayuk responded, "I shall not. What purpose would it serve for someone such as me?"

The old man spoke softly with a knowing smile, "You must go, my son. I entrust you with three hairs, each from a different-coloured horse. Burn the first, which is black, and a black stallion shall appear. Put on the clothes already prepared beneath the saddle, which shall transport you to the fortieth step. Upon your return, place the black outfit back in the box. The next day, ignite the red hair, summoning a red stallion that will carry you to the sixtieth step. Again, place the red clothes in the box upon your return. Finally, burn the white hair, and a white stallion will guide you to the top of the steps, where you may claim the hand of the princess."

With these words of guidance, the old man vanished, leaving Ayuk with the three hairs.

The following day, Esen and Badur embarked on their journey to the city, leaving Ayuk behind. Seizing the moment, Ayuk ignited the black hair, summoning the stallion. He rode atop the magnificent creature, reaching the fortieth step of the staircase. The onlookers were amazed at the mysterious knight in black.

Returning home, Ayuk carefully placed the black garments in the box beneath the saddle. As quickly as it had appeared, the black stallion disappeared. Ayuk resumed his duties, tending to the flock under Ewlik's watchful eye.

In the evening, Esen and Badur regaled Ayuk with tales of the prince in black, yearning for a glimpse of the princess. They repeated their journey the following day while Ayuk assumed the role of shepherd again.

Bidding farewell to his brothers, Ayuk set the red hair ablaze, calling forth the red stallion. He ascended to the sixtieth step, captivating the citizens with his daring feat.

Evening fell, and Esen and Badur returned to share tales of the prince in red. Ayuk listened silently, his heart brimming with a secret he could no longer contain.

As his brothers returned to the city on the third day, Ayuk ignited the white hair, summoning the majestic white stallion. Riding upon its back, Ayuk soared to the pinnacle of the staircase, reaching the eightieth step. The crowd erupted in astonishment as they beheld the prince in white.

As Ayuk approached the princess, a sense of familiarity washed over her. She saw the kindness and humility that mirrored her own in his eyes. The princess extended her hand, and Ayuk gently slipped the ring from her finger, securing their union.

The joyous crowd congratulated the prince as he triumphantly received the ring. Mounted on his faithful steed, he rode back to the humble village of Arish, where he carefully placed the enchanted clothes beneath the saddle. He then resumed his duties as a shepherd, tending to his flock.

News of the princess's marriage spread far and wide, causing great sorrow among the princes of distant lands. Realising their chance to win the princess's hand had slipped away, they despaired. Upon hearing this, the king made a solemn proclamation:

"Let it be known that the knight who successfully ascended to the eightieth step and obtained the ring shall present himself at the palace tomorrow. He shall be welcomed as my son-in-law, and the princess shall marry him."

As the evening cast its golden glow, the youngest brother observed his weary siblings returning from the city, their faces filled with bitterness and disappointment.

One grieved, "Today, a gallant prince riding a magnificent white stallion reached the eightieth step and claimed the ring. "Alas! The princess's ethereal beauty is forever lost to us."

With a heart brimming with kindness, Ayuk, the youngest brother, spoke gently, "If you possessed the ring, would you desire to become the king's son-in-law?"

"Good heavens! Ayuk, it is beyond the realm of possibility," his brothers replied. "How could a shepherd like me hold the princess's ring in my hands?"

"Here is the ring; take it to the king. You can marry the princess," Ayuk calmly offered.

Esen asked, "Where did you get this precious jewel?"

"Do not inquire about such matters. Go," Ayuk responded with a serene demeanour.

"But how can I, dressed in these tattered clothes, gain acceptance from the king? What shall I say if he questions the origins of the ring?" Esen worried.

"The king stated that whoever possesses the ring shall wed his daughter," Ayuk assured, handing the ring to his eldest brother.

Esen started to the palace the following day, clutching the ring tightly. The guards, recognising the significance of the token, granted him passage. Alone, Esen stood before the king, who received him with a hint of suspicion yet led him to his daughter's chamber.

"This is not the one who plucked the ring from my grasp," the princess proclaimed, disappointment lacing her voice.

"Guards! Seize this thief and put him into the prison!" the frustrated king commanded.

But, driven by honesty, Esen revealed the truth to the king, saying, "I obtained this ring from my brother. I know not how or where he acquired it."

The king, interested in this unexpected turn of events, ordered the soldiers to fetch Ayuk. Bound by chains, Ayuk was brought before the king, who was even more astonished. With an unwavering resolve, Ayuk proclaimed that he had received the ring from the princess's hand. Intrigued, the king led him to the chamber where the princess awaited.

"Yes, he is the one who received the ring from me. I presented it to him willingly. He is the knight who rode upon the majestic white stallion," the princess declared joyfully.

Soon after, Ayuk cleansed himself in a soothing bath and donned garments befitting the occasion. True to his word, the king fulfilled his promise, allowing Ayuk and the princess to join matrimony. Ayuk, ever generous of heart, assisted his brothers, Esen and Badur, in finding love and happiness, and they all lived joyfully ever after, their lives forever entwined in a tapestry of love and fortune.

Swallow and Kutluk

A child named Kutluk dwelled not long ago, blessed with a heart brimming with kindness. Beneath the porch in his yard, a humble swallow had chosen to build its nest. Throughout the summer, four tiny swallows grew within that cosy haven, their curious eyes gazing upon a garden adorned with grapevines and the melodies of songbirds.

One fateful day, as Kutluk returned home from the fields at noon, he discovered a baby swallow lying helpless in the centre of the porch. The little bird had fallen from its nest. Tenderly, Kutluk cradled it in his palm, noticing that one of its delicate legs was in a severe state. Filled with compassion, he caressed its wings, kissed its head, and gently rubbed its weary eyes, fearing it may be dropped from its tiny sanctuary.

"What troubles your feet, little one?" he asked softly.

The mother swallowed, soaring above the walls, looked upon Kutluk, and chirped, "Cheep, chirrup, we know not the cause. Pray, tell me what afflicts my offspring."

Kutluk shared his assumption about the mishap: "The baby swallows quarrelled within the nest, and alas, this poor soul tumbled and broke its leg."

Hearing this, the mother glanced at her child and sighed, "Did we not beg you to live in peace and harmony? What shall we do if you disregard our counsel? Oh, dear heavens, what shall we do?"

Kutluk turned his gaze and replied, "I require a thread, a pair of slender twigs; they may heal its leg..." He hastened to his mother, who provided him with thread, a pinch of cotton, and two small twigs. He carefully bound the baby swallow's legs, then ascended to the nest, gently placing the little one back within its snug abode. A sense of triumph filled Kutluk's heart as he completed his noble task.

"Well done, well done, let us not forget," the mother swallow trilled joyfully, expressing her gratitude to Kutluk. "cheep, chirrup, now it is better." Moreover, she calmed her heart and flew away again, seeking grains to feed her beloved offspring.

Days passed, and the baby swallow's legs mended, enabling it to join its parents and soar through the skies again. As winter approached, the swallows embarked on their journey south, bidding farewell to snow and ice. The following year, as spring blossomed, painting the world with vibrant hues, the swallows returned, building their nests, and the children revelled in the beauty of their splendid garden.

While Kutluk sat beneath the porch, he awaited the swallow's arrival. Recognising the familiar bird, Kutluk chuckled with delight. Alas, as the swallow dropped the seed from its beak, it tumbled.

"Plant the seed," the swallow urged.

It was a watermelon seed, and Kutluk swiftly picked it up, cradling it in his hand. He hurried to the field, choosing a spot to sow the seed. With unwavering dedication, Kutluk tended to the seedling, his heart filled with hope. Week by week, he witnessed the watermelon vines sprout and flourish within his patch, diligently watering them. Astonishingly, the watermelons seemed to grow accelerated, evoking great anticipation within Kutluk's heart.

"How mouthwatering they shall be," he whispered, basking in the sun's warmth while watching the juicy fruits ripen.

Finally, the day arrived when the watermelons seemed perfectly ripe, and Kutluk yearned to taste their sweet flesh. Oh, what a splendid sight they were! One watermelon stood out, colossal and magnificent. Kutluk tapped it gently, sensing its ripeness, then rushed home, believing it too weighty to carry alone.

"Father! The watermelons have ripened, and one among them is extraordinary and immense," Kutluk beseeched his parents. "The grand watermelon is heavy beyond measure. Let us fashion a stretcher to carry it home swiftly."

So, with the help of his father, Kutluk carefully positioned the watermelon upon a makeshift stretcher. As they began their journey homeward, several passersby, including Kutluk's mother, joined them, lending their strength to the arduous task. Only then did they successfully transport the mammoth watermelon to their dwelling.

Kutluk's mind raced with thoughts of quenching his family's thirst with the luscious fruit. With eager anticipation, he sliced open the watermelon. To his astonishment, a cascade of golden seeds spilt forth, resembling a mound of precious coins.

Together, they savoured the delicious fruit, sharing it with their neighbours. Each voice resounded with delight as they indulged, exclaiming, "Truly remarkable! A good deed brings forth another!"

However, their neighbour's son, the envious and greedy Baki, upon hearing of Kutluk's fortune, harboured a deep longing to amass riches of his own.

When spring arrived, and the baby swallows emerged from their nests, Baki devised a wicked plan. He stole one of the baby swallows and purposely bound its wing with a small twig, feigning concern for the bird's injury.

Shortly after, the mother swallow returned to her nest, witnessing the betrayal and discerning the truth. Her children, distressed, recounted the tale of the deceit.

The mother swallow reassured them solemnly, saying, "cheep, chirrup, fret not, my darlings." Tenderly, she untied the bandage from her offspring's wing and soared back to the fields for sustenance.

Days turned into weeks, and the swallows embarked on their journey south, seeking warmth in the late autumn. Meanwhile, Baki spent his winter days consumed by fantasies of golden watermelon seeds. With the arrival of spring, he anxiously monitored his nest, eagerly awaiting the swallows' return. Finally, a swallow arrived and dropped a watermelon seed into his garden. Overwhelmed with joy, Baki promptly buried the seed in the ground, counting the days until it sprouted and bore fruit.

One day, as he gazed upon his garden, a colossal watermelon hung from the vine, signalling its ripeness. Baki eagerly sliced open the fruit, but to his horror, the seeds swarmed around him like vengeful bees, relentlessly pursuing him.

"Allah, alas!" he cried, seeking refuge and covering himself in mud.

A crowd gathered, inquiring, "What has befallen you?"

With a defeated gaze, Baki uttered, "I have received my just deserts."

And the mother swallowed, with a hint of satisfaction in her voice, declared, "Cheep, chirrup, evildoers reap what they sow."

Man's Due

Once upon a time, in a land of friendships and disputes, there lived two young companions, Tursun and Turdi. They found themselves entangled in a debate over the concept of a man's due and whether it could be delayed. Tursun, eager for answers, asked, "Does fate ever delay what is owed to a man?"

Turdi replied with wisdom beyond his years, "Oh, my dear friend, the passing of months and years may blur the passage of time, but karma, like a faithful companion, always returns."

Tursun, sceptical yet intrigued, challenged Turdi, saying, "But how can you prove such a notion? Can you illustrate it as vividly as the sun illuminates the sky?"

With a twinkle in his eye, Turdi began to spin a tale, transporting them to a bustling city that embraced nature's beauty. "In this enchanting city," Turdi started, "there dwelled a great miser whose heart was tarnished by dishonesty and greed."

He continued, painting a vivid picture of a carpenter who toiled tirelessly for the miser for five long years, crafting masterful works with his skilful hands. When the carpenter's time ended, he departed from this world, leaving behind a massive sum of wages he had not been paid. The miser, while burying the carpenter's body, never thought of finding the carpenter's next of kin to pay his wages for five years.

The miser, unburdened by obligation, relaxed in the freedom he had attained. However, destiny, ever vigilant, had more in store for him. One day, the miser embarked on a business venture to a neighbouring city, carrying thirty gleaming gold nuggets secured in a drawstring bag tied around his waist. As the sweating heat bore down upon him, fatigue beckoned him to rest beneath the shade of a towering poplar tree near a flowing river.

However, the heavy gold nuggets weighed uncomfortably against his body, denying him rest. He reluctantly untied the bag with a sigh. He hung it from a sturdy branch, thinking, "Surely, no one would dare to journey into the desert carrying such a precious burden." Finally, overcome by weariness, he surrendered to sleep, drifting into slumber beneath the blue sky.

As dusk faded into the night, the miser awoke with a start, realising the passing of time. Panic gripped him, and he hastily mounted his horse, fleeing from the scene. Unbeknownst to him, a carpenter's apprentice, carrying his carpentry tools, sought rest beneath the same tree.

Weary, he leaned against its trunk when his gaze fell upon the drawstring bag nestled amidst the branches.

Curiosity piqued, the young apprentice rose slowly and retrieved the bag. With trembling hands, he untied it, revealing a cascade of pure gold. Overwhelmed with joy, he murmured, "Oh, dear God, this is your gift to me!" Nevertheless, a sudden realisation halted his celebration. "Surely, the one who lost these golden nuggets must be filled with despair," he pondered.

Filled with a sense of duty, the apprentice embarked on a journey to the city on foot, carrying the precious gold to deliver to the wise judge, the Qadi. Hours turned into an eternity as he went to the town, searching for the esteemed Qadi's presence.

Meanwhile, the miser, plagued by anxiety, retraced his steps, desperately seeking his misplaced treasure. It was beneath the same tree that he encountered an elderly man calmly resting with a water-filled gourd in his possession. The miser, his heart racing, scoured the area, the drawstring bag nowhere in sight.

Turning to the old man, he questioned, "Have you seen something amiss? I had hung an item upon this very branch, which has vanished. Pray, tell me, have you caught sight of it?"

The old man, serene, replied, "I have not laid eyes on it, my brother. Since I arrived and settled beneath this tree, I have not ventured near its branches."

Doubt seeped into the miser's voice as he implored, "Swear upon your honesty, and I shall reward you handsomely."

The old man, firm in his innocence, responded, "I speak the truth, for I have not seen what you seek."

Frustration bubbling within him, the miser warned, "If you persist in falsehood, I shall escort you to the esteemed Qadi, and justice shall prevail!"

The miser led the old man to the Qadi, determined to seek justice for his lost treasure. The Qadi, a discerning judge of character, ordered a thorough investigation into the matter, eager to uncover the truth and ensure justice prevailed.

At long last, on foot, the young carpenter found himself face-to-face with the judge, who was already handling reports of lost and found gold nuggets.

After meticulously examining the evidence and testimonies, the Qadi reached a verdict that would resonate with the crowd. In a public proclamation, he revealed that the carpenter's apprentice was, in fact, the son of the deceased carpenter who had toiled diligently under the miser's employ. Moreover, the old man harboured a dark secret—he was the very robber who had stolen and slain the miser's father.

In the wake of this revelation, justice unfolded its wings, granting each party their rightful dues. The carpenter's son, finally reunited with his father's hard-earned wages, felt a profound sense of closure and peace. The miser, chastised for his carelessness with another man's wealth, faced the consequences of his actions. Furthermore, the old man, burdened by his past misdeeds, met the fate he had long evaded.

Turdi concluded his tale with a knowing smile, turning to Tursun and affirming, "You see, my dear friend, karma is an eternal force. Its wheels forever turn, ensuring that virtuous and wicked deeds return to their rightful owners."

Tursun's doubts quelled, and his heart, touched by the power of destiny, nodded in agreement and whispered, "Truly, karma always comes back." And so, their minds were enlightened, and their friendship fortified by the timeless wisdom they had uncovered together.

Fish and Fox

Long ago, in the broad and glistening waters of Turum Lake, countless fish lived, their lives flowing with the gentle rhythm of the lake's currents. But alas, fortune turned against them, and the lake began to dry up, its life-giving waters shrinking a little more with each passing day.

One fateful day, as the sun cast its golden rays upon the parched land, a fox with a hungry appetite wandered near the lonely lake. This cunning creature had endured three long days without tasting any meat, and his hunger gnawed at him fiercely. His keen eyes detected a fish lying helplessly in the mud, a pitiful sight amidst the dwindling water.

Driven by the primal urge to satisfy his hunger, the fox entered the lake, his heart filled with hope. Witnessing the approaching predator, the fish trembled in fear, its body wriggling with desperation.

As the fox drew nearer, the fish, gathering all its courage, regained its composure and addressed the fox in a trembling voice, "Oh, dear brother of the forest, do you intend to eat me?"

With a mischievous glint, the fox smirked and replied, "Indeed, brother fish, my stomach growls with hunger, for days have passed since I last tasted nourishment. But fear not, for even if I were to spare you, this dwindling lake would inevitably dry up, leading to your death."

Realising the direness of its situation, the fish pondered for a moment before presenting a cunning proposition. "Very well, if it is my fate to become your meal, I beg you to consider this. Feasting upon me with this mud clinging to my scales will surely cause great distress to your stomach. Therefore, I pray you, dear fox, cleanse me thoroughly before consuming my flesh."

The fox, intrigued by the fish's suggestion, thought it wise and agreed. He carried the fish to a serene lake in a green valley, its pristine waters shining with purity.

As the fish's body touched the refreshing water, a surge of vitality coursed through its being. Seizing this fleeting moment of freedom, it unleashed its tail with all its might, striking the fox's eyes with a force that brought forth a cry of pain. Startled and disoriented, the fox lost its grip on the slippery prey, and the fish slipped from its jaws, triumphantly plunging back into the sanctuary of the water.

Fuming anger and a greedy thirst for revenge, the fox longed to plunge into the lake's depths to retrieve its stolen prize. But, alas, the fox had never learned to swim. So, with great reluctance, it swallowed its pride and fury, forever accepting its bitter loss.

Brilliant Chimenkhan

In a time long past, in a land where dreams and wonders intertwined, there lived a man named Bogu. He was neither rich nor poor but content in the simple life of the middle class. Known for his wisdom and wealth of experiences, Bogu became a guiding light for the villagers, who often sought his counsel in times of need. His words of wisdom would unfold and shape their lives like ripples in a still pond.

Bogu had a beloved daughter named Chimenkhan, whom he cherished dearly and taught with great care. In a village where proper schools were a distant dream, Bogu, along with other kind-hearted souls, taught the children the sacred arts of reading and writing. Chimenkhan, a bright and eager learner, thrived under her father's guidance and often contributed her insights, her young mind brimming with wisdom.

One fateful day, a summons arrived from the regal halls of King Tekish's court, carrying whispers of Bogu's scholarly prowess. The king, aware of this educated man dwelling among his subjects, sought to put his wisdom to the test. With an air of regal authority, King Tekish addressed Bogu, "I have heard tales of your knowledge and ability to provide sensible counsel. If these rumours bear truth, I shall present you with four questions. Should you unravel their mysteries within three sunsets, I shall bestow upon you a role as a trusted consultant within my palace. However, failure to do so shall invite you to return to where you belong."

Bound by the king's decree and unable to challenge his authority, Bogu accepted with a respectful nod and replied, "As you wish, Your Majesty. I shall follow your words."

The king then revealed his questions, each as mysterious as a hidden moon behind the clouds. "First," said King Tekish, "tell me, what is the swiftest thing in the world? Second, what is the most bitter? Third, what is the sweetest? And lastly, what is the greatest hardship of all?"

With a heavy heart, Bogu returned to his home, the weight of the king's riddles pressing upon him. He pondered the questions, but their answers seemed as elusive as shadows in the night. As the days passed and the sun set twice, Bogu grew weary and troubled, fearing he might fail the king's test.

The sun's golden radiance waned, and the moon ascended its throne in the sky, yet Bogu found no solace in his search for enlightenment. The hours slipped away like sands through an hourglass, and despair began to cast its shadow upon his weary soul. How could he unravel these enigmas and emerge unscathed?

Desperate for answers, Bogu gathered his friends and shared his plight, "I have often offered you advice in times of need. Now, I ask for your wisdom, for the king has set a challenge I cannot solve alone before me."

His friends, eager to help, asked, "What troubles you so, dear Bogu?"

Bogu explained the king's questions, and they pondered the riddles. One friend declared, "The wind is surely the swiftest, for it races across the land without pause." Another countered, "No, a bullet is faster still, as quick as lightning." Yet another suggested, "The chilli pepper is the most bitter, for its fiery taste burns the tongue."

More voices joined in, offering different answers: poison for bitterness, stones for hardness, etc. But amid this flurry of ideas, Chimenkhan, who had been quietly listening, spoke up with calm conviction, "Dear Father and friends, you have all spoken wisely. But in my view, the swiftest thing is the mind, which travels anywhere instantly. The most bitter thing is the heart of an enemy, where hatred festers. The sweetest is the love between brothers, and the greatest hardship is poverty, which steals dignity and hope."

Her words fell like gentle rain, and as her friends and father listened, they knew her answers rang true. Hope blossomed in Bogu's heart, and with renewed courage, he returned to the king's court the next day.

Standing before King Tekish, Bogu humbly recited Chimenkhan's answers. "The swiftest thing is the mind, the most bitter is the heart of an enemy, the sweetest is the bond of brotherhood, and the hardest burden is poverty."

King Tekish was pleased but curious. "Did you find these answers on your own, or were they given to you by another?" he asked.

Bogu, valuing honesty over pride, replied, "Your Majesty, these answers come from my daughter, Chimenkhan, whose wisdom far surpasses my own."

Intrigued, the king ordered, "Bring her to me, but beware—she must not enter the palace nor stand at its entrance."

Bogu returned home with heavy news, and embracing Chimenkhan, he told her of the king's command. Yet Chimenkhan, undaunted, comforted her father, "Do not worry, Father. I will go to the king and see what must be done."

Together, they went to the palace, and Chimenkhan stopped at the threshold, one foot inside and one out, honouring the king's command. She bowed and addressed the king, "Your Majesty, I stand here as you decreed, neither inside nor outside, as you did not specify where I should be."

Impressed by her cleverness, the king invited her in and asked, "Tell me, young one, how did you come to such an understanding?"

Chimenkhan bowed gracefully and spoke, "I learned that the mind is the swiftest, for it can journey through all of time and space in a mere thought. I saw bitterness in enemies' hearts who met tragic ends in their conflict. I found sweetness in the embrace of brothers who reconciled after a quarrel. And when we had nothing to offer to guests who came to our home in my father's absence, I understood that poverty is the greatest hardship, for it leaves us powerless to fulfil even the simplest kindness."

King Tekish, moved by Chimenkhan's wisdom, decided to nurture her gifts. He arranged for her to attend the finest school in the kingdom and welcomed Bogu into his service, valuing the knowledge that came from such humble roots. And so, Bogu and Chimenkhan's lives were forever changed as they brought light and learning to all those they touched, proving that even the most straightforward hearts can hold the greatest truths.

What is God doing?

Once upon a time, in a humble village nestled at the edge of a grand kingdom, there lived a poor man named Yoksul. He dwelt in a shabby hut, clothed in tattered rags, and often sighed at the world's great injustices. One fateful day, the king returned from a long journey. Yoksul, with eyes wide in wonder, beheld the king draped in robes of the finest linen, his head crowned with a veil adorned in gold and rubies that sparkled like the stars.

"Surely, the heavens have woven different fates for kings and common folk," thought Yoksul, his heart heavy with longing. After a moment's pause, he quietly turned and went.

Yet Yoksul's curiosity was not quickly quelled. The next day, he ventured to the palace gates and humbly asked the king, "Your Majesty, may I know the name of this day?"

Surprised by the question's simplicity, the king announced the day's name to all who gathered. But Yoksul, undeterred, returned the next day to ask once more. Perplexed by the poor man's persistence, the king finally asked, "Why do you trouble yourself with this question daily? Have you no better task to fill your time?"

With unwavering resolve, Yoksul bowed low and replied, "My lord, I have nought to occupy my days but to unravel the names bestowed upon them."

The king, puzzled, asked, "But what use is there in determining the names of the days?"

Yoksul, recalling his earlier encounter with the king, spoke earnestly. "When I saw you return, resplendent in your robes and laden with riches, a thought stirred in my heart. Despite the endless toil of my family and me, we often hunger and shiver in the cold of night. It seemed that God has ordained separate fates for the monarch and the meek."

Intrigued by Yoksul's musings, the king asked, "Do you see a difference in our days, then?"

Yoksul, without a hint of fear, answered, "No, my lord. The first three days of this week have passed just the same, and I expect no change in the days to come."

The king, deeply moved by Yoksul's plight, reached into his pocket and, with a generous hand, gave the poor man a fistful of gold. His act of kindness resonated with the courtiers, but the king's vizier looked on, his heart ablaze with envy and greed.

Later, the Vizier approached the king, his face darkened by displeasure. The king, noticing his advisor's troubled countenance, asked, "What ails you, my faithful vizier?"

With a bitter tone, the Vizier replied, "Your Majesty, though it seems a trifle to you, acquiring such gold is no easy feat for men like us."

The king, unfazed, replied kindly, "If this gold burdens your conscience, you may seek to reclaim it, but let no harm come to the man. And bring him not before me again."

Determined to reclaim the gold, the Vizier mounted his sleek black stallion and pursued Yoksul. Catching up to him, he called out, "Stop, poor man! I have a question for you, and if you answer correctly, I shall not touch your gold. But if you fail, it shall be mine once more."

Sensing the Vizier's malice, Yoksul stood firm and said, "Ask your question, good sir."

The Vizier paused, took a deep breath, and asked, "Tell me, what is God doing now?"

Before answering, Yoksul proposed a test. "Dismount your horse and remove your fine clothes. Let me don your robes and ride your steed. Only then will I answer, for I wish to speak as you do, and you shall bear witness as I do now. If you refuse, we shall go to the king."

The Vizier, anxious to preserve his pride, reluctantly agreed. But he warned, "Do as you wish, but if your answer disappoints, the gold shall be mine."

Quickly, Yoksul swapped his rags for the Vizier's finery and mounted the grand horse. The Vizier, standing in his undergarments, pleaded, "Speak now! Tell me, what is God doing?"

Yoksul, with calm confidence, replied, "In this very moment, God has made the rider a walker and the walker a rider. Do you wish to ask more?"

The Vizier, utterly astounded by Yoksul's wisdom, could only stammer, "My horse, my horse!" He gazed at Yoksul, humbled by the poor man's profound insight.

Yoksul, taking the reins in hand, smiled and said, "Cease your chase, dear Vizier." With a swift turn, he galloped away, leaving the astonished Vizier far behind.

And so, the Vizier stood in his simple garments, pondering the swift turn of fate that had befallen him. In that moment, he learned a great truth: that the wheels of fortune turn for all and that wisdom can spring from the humblest of hearts. And Yoksul, now dressed in silk robes, rode onward, a testament to the ever-turning whims of destiny.

Treasure Mountain

Once upon a time, in the heart of a land steeped in ancient tales and whispered secrets, stood a magnificent peak known to all as the "Treasure Mountain." Its towering slopes glittered in the sunlight, dazed with veins of gold, silver, and rubies, along with rare gems that no human eye had fully seen. Cloaked in mist and legend, this majestic mountain had never been conquered, for no man had ever climbed its formidable heights.

In the shadow of this mountain, in a picturesque village, there lived a master jeweller named Atat. Dreams of great wealth drove him. He spent his days hunched over his workbench, fashioning fine jewels while secretly longing for the treasures hidden on the unreachable summit. But no matter how much he dreamed, Atat remained tethered to the ground, ever yearning, never attaining.

One fateful evening, as Atat sat in his modest shop, an old man, bent and weathered, entered and made him a peculiar offer. "Would you like to buy my marvellous sack?" the old man asked. "With but a whisper of 'Fly,

fly,' this sack shall soar to any height or distance, though beware—it cannot return to the earth."

Intrigued and eager to seize any chance that might bring him closer to his dreams, Atat bought the enchanted sack without hesitation. As twilight painted the village in hues of purple and gold, Atat returned home. He gazed at the roof of his humble abode, filled the sack with a heavy stone, and commanded, "Fly to the roof, fly to the roof!" And so, the sack obeyed, lifting itself and its burden to the rooftop. Atat's heart leapt with joy; at last, he had found a means to reach the summit of Treasure Mountain.

The following day, Atat went to the bustling labour market and hired a firm, willing worker. He treated the man kindly for several days, offering him food and lodging. Then, when the moment was ripe, Atat revealed the secret of the magical sack and cunningly persuaded the worker to step inside. With a sly grin, Atat shouted, "Fly to the top, fly to the top!" And the sack rose, carrying the worker up, up, up, toward the gleaming summit. As the worker exited the bag, Atat said, "Fill the sack with gold and cast it down to me, and I shall return you safely to the earth." Trusting Atat, the worker did as he was told, sending the sack brimming with gold to the ground below. But Atat, consumed by greed, seized the sack and fled to the city, never looking back. The poor worker, left stranded on the mountain, soon perished, lost and alone.

Time and again, Atat repeated his wicked scheme, luring young men with promises of fortune only to abandon them on the mountain's deadly heights. His insatiable greed lost many souls, their bones mingling with the jewels they had sought.

One day, as Atat hung around the market for another unsuspecting victim, his boastful words caught the ear of a clever orphan named Botuk. The boy approached the jeweller, his eyes shining with innocence and cunning. "Kind sir," Botuk said, "I am called Botuk and seek work. Will you not take me on as your servant?"

Intrigued by the boy's boldness, Atat agreed and led Botuk to the mountain's base. With practised deception, he instructed the boy to climb into the enchanted sack. As Botuk hesitated, Atat's grin grew wider, his thoughts racing ahead to the riches awaited. Botuk flew to the top of the mountain and did what Atat asked for. Atat left Botuk on the mountain, just as he had done with the others, and departed.

Botuk's eyes, sharp and perceptive, fell upon the scattered jewels and bones strewn along the mountain path. At that moment, he understood the treachery at play—the mountain was littered with the remnants of those who had fallen victim to Atat's greed.

Botuk's heart burned with anger, but he bided his time, subsisting on rainwater and wild herbs as he plotted his escape. He vowed to the heavens that if he survived, he would bring justice upon the wicked jeweller who had left so many to perish.

One day, as the sun gleamed upon the treacherous peak, Botuk spied a river far below, winding its way through the valley. He hurled himself from the mountain with a courageous leap, plunging into the swift current. Miraculously, the waters carried him safely to the riverbank, battered but alive. Determined, Botuk made his way home, changed from his ragged clothes, cleaned himself up, and prepared to face the days ahead. He knew his moment for retribution was near.

In time, Botuk returned to the labour market, blending in among the throngs of workers. Before long, Atat arrived, oblivious to the storm brewing in Botuk's heart. The boy manoeuvred himself into Atat's view, and soon enough, the jeweller hired him, planning once more to exploit the magic of the flying sack.

The following day dawned bright, but an eerie fog soon rolled in, cloaking the world in mystery. Botuk accompanied Atat to the jeweller's house, where they spent a seemingly ordinary evening. Yet Botuk's mind was anything but ordinary, filled with thoughts of justice and retribution. The following day, they journeyed to the mountain's base, where Atat, ever eager, instructed Botuk to enter the sack. "Come, boy," Atat said with a sly smile. "Step inside, and I shall lift you to the mountaintop and bring you back once your task is done."

But Botuk, sparkling with wit, replied, "Uncle, why don't you show me how it's done?"

Atat, eager to demonstrate his supposed prowess, slipped into the sack. Seizing his moment, Botuk swiftly tightened the sack's mouth and commanded, "Fly to the top, fly to the top!" The enchanted sack obeyed, whisking the deceitful jeweller to the mountain's lonely peak.

As Atat stumbled out of the sack, bewildered and afraid, Botuk's voice echoed through the heights. "You vile man! You tricked me and so many others into this dangerous trap. But now, it is your turn to face the consequences of your greed. One wrong does deserve another."

Leaving Atat stranded atop the mountain, Botuk turned his back on the jeweller's pleas. He mounted Atat's mule and rode back to the city, his heart alight with the glow of justice served. Botuk immediately approached the local authorities, revealing Atat's heinous crimes and deceitful deeds.

Thus, the villagers learned of Atat's betrayal, and justice was finally revealed. Botuk became a symbol of courage and righteousness, forever remembered as the boy who conquered Treasure Mountain—not through greed, but through the triumph of a just and noble heart.

Printed in Great Britain
by Amazon